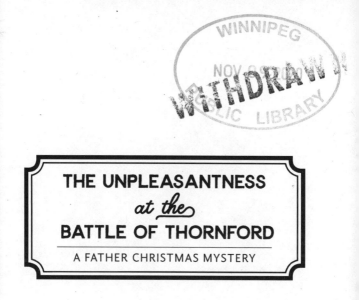

THE UNPLEASANTNESS
at the
BATTLE OF THORNFORD

A FATHER CHRISTMAS MYSTERY

THE UNPLEASANTNESS
at the
BATTLE OF THORNFORD

A FATHER CHRISTMAS MYSTERY

C.C. BENISON

AT BAY
press

WINNIPEG

The Unpleasantness at the Battle of Thornford
A Father Christmas Mystery

Copyright © November 2020 Douglas Whiteway

Design by M. C. Joudrey and Matthew Stevens
Layout by Matthew Stevens and M. C. Joudrey
Cover illustration by M. C. Joudrey
Cover design and layout by M. C. Joudrey and Matthew Stevens

Published by At Bay Press November 2020

Library and Archives Canada cataloguing in publication is available upon request.

ISBN 978-1-988168-41-8

Printed and bound in Canada.

First Edition

10 9 8 7 6 5 4 3 2 1

atbaypress.com

This book is printed on acid free paper that is 100% recycled ancient forest friendly (100% post-consumer recycled).

Inhabitants of Thornford Regis

Rev'd Tom Christmas	Vicar of the parish
Miranda Christmas	His daughter
Florence Daintrey	Retired civil servant
Venice Daintrey	Her sister-in-law
Jeanette Neels	Co-owner of Thorn Barton farm
Roger Pattimore	Owner of Pattimore's, the village shop
Madrun Prowse	Vicarage housekeeper
Jago Prowse	Her brother, owner of Thorn Cross Garage
Tamara and Kerra	His daughters
Eric Swan	Licensee of the Church House Inn
Belinda Swan	His wife
Daniel, Lucy, Emily, and Jack	Their children
Mark Tucker	Solicitor

Visitors to Thornford Regis

Colin Blessing	Detective Sergeant, Totnes CID
Derek Bliss	Detective Inspector, Totnes CID
Rev'd Barbara Coaker	Vicar of Hamlyn Ferrers
Elise Coaker	Her sister

Others

Dania Bloczynski	Housecleaner
Lily	Her daughter
Elkanah Mayhew	Insurance broker
Julia Rose	Tom's sister-in-law

In memory of the Reverend Dave Treby

1

Saturday

It occurred to Tom Christmas that some country events were really very odd. This one in particular, he thought, surveying the costumed folk wandering about Hailstone Field.

He had been called upon to lend his vicarly presence to a reenactment of the Battle of Thornford, which had been fought in 1645 between the usual suspects, the Royalists and the Parliamentarians, in the Civil War. That the battle had taken place in December and the reenactment in August, when the kids were off school and the weather more likely favourable, suggested that this was no zealous approach to capturing authenticity. Madrun, his redoubtable housekeeper, proclaimed the Battle of Thornford a shining beacon in the history of the county (or some such thing) but Tom, glancing through regional histories previous incumbents had parked in the vicarage study, was hard pressed to find mention of it, other than a footnoted reference in one tome to a short engagement in a field between the village of Hamlyn Ferrers, which stood for Parliament, and nearby Thornford, which stood for the King. (The "Regis" would come one hundred and fifty years later when the Prince Regent spent a congenial few days with his mistress at Thornridge House, built by his favourite architect, John Nash). It appeared to be rather less a "battle" than a "skirmish" or, perhaps, an "incident" or—really—little more than an "unpleasantness" as the weary locals dragged themselves out for a final bash at one another in the protracted war that divided England in the seventeenth century.

The reenactment was, of course, a fundraiser, with monies shared between charities of the two villages. On the periphery of the field were the customary delights to relieve the hoi polloi of their pounds and pence—a beer tent and a barbeque and a candy-floss stall and cow-pat sweepstakes and much else—but the central event was the recreation of the historic clash with floppy-hatted Cavaliers to one side and saucepan-helmetted Roundheads to the other. Tom should have been alerted by the unusual show of force by St. John Ambulance on the periphery of the makeshift car park or by the slipping away as the hour approached of mothers with young children, but he wasn't. He didn't recognise many of the Thornfordites and wondered that the village had so many big fit lads, saying so to Barbara Coaker, the new vicar of All Saints in Hamlyn, a spinster as tightly buttoned up as her cassock, who cast him an ambiguous glance and said nothing. He had expected some sort of choreographed spectacle, with cannon, muskets and pikes, and with period dress in Royalist gleam and Puritan drab. He'd seen one on TV and it was quite grand, with lots of swaggering and shouting and gun smoke (fake, of course) and noble horses, and it was quite silly, too, what with the dead, as such, rising from their eternal slumber to bow before a captivated audience.

But the reenactment of the Battle of Thornford was little different than a pub brawl. Participants were minimally costumed, horses there were none, and armaments there were few—a pike here, a musket there. After a short Communion service from the two vicars, the unpredictable English sky let loose a brief barrage of rain while each side set on the other with a fiercesome roar, struggling in the churning mud—fists and feet the weapons of choice. Startled out of his skin, he shot forward to enter the melee to try and put a stop to the brutality, but one of the St. John Ambulance grabbed his arm and said in a thick West Country accent, "You never mind, Vicar, you let them lads have at it." And he did, as options were none. The onlookers, including the vicar of Hamlyn, a woman plain as a pikestaff, cheered and booed with gusto and, before long, Tom felt himself unmoored from the bonds of adult decorum, slipping back to an adolescent self where schoolyard altercations stoked primitive bloodlust. His own response horrified him, and this was only partly mitigated when he realised—and this was confirmed by others later—that the reenactors were mostly ringers, enthusiastic amateur pugilists, happy to be proxies in this peculiar local catharsis. Even now, more than three and a half centuries after the Civil War, some of the older residents of Thornford still dismissed the yeomanry of Hamlyn Ferrers as "Roundheads." Memory ran deep in the countryside.

Tom returned to the vicarage late that afternoon in a state of profound unhappiness. He found Madrun in the kitchen removing a gooseberry tart from the Aga. She glanced at him over the tops of her glasses, frowned, and reached to put the kettle on the hob. She had come

3

to know her employer's deep silences portended some sort of crisis, spiritual or otherwise, but it was often a task unbottling the bottled-up details. Mr. Christmas prized circumspection and disdained anything he considered tittle-tattle. Madrun considered this a most unwise and impractical approach to village life. A nice cup of tea, she thought, might loosen his tongue. If only the gooseberry tart weren't so scorching hot, she could put that in front of him, too, with some clotted cream, but alas…

"Did you find the battle to your liking, Mr. Christmas," she asked lightly, opening a tin of lemon biscuits instead.

"I most certainly did not. I can't think the last time I witnessed such an appalling spectacle."

"I grant it is a little rough around the edges. When I was a girl—"

"Rough around the edges?" Tom interrupted, absently taking a proffered biscuit. "Mrs. Prowse, someone *died* at this year's Battle of Thornford."

"But, Mr. Christmas, many of them 'die'. It is a battle, after all."

"No, no. I mean die as in …" Tom groped for an explanation. "As in cease to be. Life force vanished. Meet your Maker. That sort of thing."

"You mean … someone *died*?"

"Got it in one."

"But how?"

"It's awful. Someone was stabbed with a pike."

"In the battle?"

"No. That's the odd part." Tom bit into the biscuit as Madrun placed the teapot in front of him. "*After* the battle—if you can call that fracas a battle. Barbara stumbled across this poor man behind the trees off the car park, in Morchard Wood. You might know Barbara—vicar of All Saints. She was in the woods to … well, never mind. Let's just say the beverages were copious and the portaloos insufficient. Anyway, everyone seemed to want to call it an accident.

"People do stab themselves, Mr. Christmas. I remember when—"

"Yes," Tom interrupted again, "people do stab themselves, I'm sure, but *not* with a pike. Pikes are ten feet long—at the shortest"

"They *are* pointed at one end, with metal."

"But you'd have to run at it. Or fall on it. Is that possible?" Tom asked rhetorically. He considered the placement of the body, when he'd gone to look, and shuddered in memory: The man was pinned to the ground at the neck, the steel point and part of the staff ripped through his flesh and pointed at the sky, the rest of the staff broken beneath his body. Blood pooled like a crimson nimbus around his head. It was a ghastly sight. And there was one other detail, but he thought he'd keep it from his housekeeper. "I think they're calling it an accident because no one wants to credit that it may *not* be an accident. They don't want Health and Safety to shut the reenactment down for good. And it should be shut down."

Madrun lifted the teapot. "Who was it who died?"

"That's another odd bit. No one seemed to know at first. But then most of the reenactors didn't seem to belong to either village. It was quite peculiar."

"King or Parliament?" Madrun poured the tea.

"The deceased? Parliament. He was wearing one of those pot helmets over his head."

"Hamlyn, then. He would be connected to Hamlyn Ferrers."

5

"If any of them were connected to anything." Tom lifted the teacup to his lips. "Finally some … kid in a Cavalier hat gave me a name."

Madrun picked up a biscuit and regarded him with avid curiosity.

"Well, I suppose it will be public knowledge before long." Tom wished she would sit down rather than hover so. "Oddly, the name clanged a bell. But perhaps it's because the name sounds like yours, Mrs. Prowse. The poor man's name was … let me think, Charles Rouse."

Tom observed the biscuit stop half way to Madrun's mouth. "Charles Rouse? *Charley* Rouse?"

"Clanging a bell for you, too?"

"Yes."

"Which bell then?"

"My brother's … brother-in-law was … is named Charles Rouse. Maureen's brother."

"Oh?" Tom observed a paleness settle on his house-keeper's face.

"But he hasn't been seen in … eight? nine? years."

"It can't be an uncommon name, Mrs. Prowse. They may be several Charles Rouses about."

"What did he look like?"

Tom thought back. He was quite tall, for one thing, or would have been had he been standing. The helmet obscured much of the man's head. In the horror of the moment, he only took a quick glimpse of the face below. Thinnish, narrowish, a bit pointy at chin and nose? Hardly a "round head." Eyes shut, so no salient detail there. Late forties, early fifties? It was a rough guess. He gave an edited version to Madrun.

"I shall have to tell Jago."

"Your brother?" Tom watched with perplexity as

Madrun's eyes darted to the kitchen phone. "Then you're certain this is your Charles Rouse."

"Certainly not *my* Charles Rouse, Mr. Christmas. But he's certainly *that* Charles Rouse."

"Can you be sure?"

"The Charley Rouse who lived at Hamlyn Ferrers was very fond of two things. One of them was the Civil War. Mad about reenactments and such."

"Oh? And what was the other?"

Madrun's lips drew to a pinch. "I can't say."

2

Sunday

Tom pushed the event from his mind Saturday evening as he polished his sermon for the next day and rehearsed it in front of Powell and Gloria, the vicarage cats, in his study. But Sunday morning's seven o'clock newscast on Radio Devon served as reminder. Charles Rouse's death was the last, brief item, included at all, Tom suspected, more for its uncommonness than for its consequence. As victim, Rouse wasn't named, pending notification of family, and of course there would be an inquest, as there always was when death was anything but nature taking its course, but the newscast's seeming presumption of accidental death troubled him.

He recalled the scene again as he was shaving, particularly the detail he'd kept from Madrun. Charley's flies had been open and his penis, not unreasonably given the circumstance, had retracted like a turtle's head. He had been splayed awkwardly upon a little hummock in the woods floor; that, plus the angle of the pike's spike end through his neck suggested he had been peeing against a tree, somehow lost his footing, and pitched backwards

9

onto the spike. A horrible end to a life. But at the time he wondered: how might the pike have been positioned for this very horrible end?

Barbara had been greatly shaken by her discovery, and once Tom felt he could leave the scene in responsible hands he led her away to the gruff St. John's Ambulance man who covered her in an emergency blanket. When her teeth stopped chattering and she could get a few coherent words out, the words were "badger hole." When she neared Charley, to see if there was something she could do, before she realised he was dead, she'd nearly tripped over it. She reasoned Charley had secured his pike in the depths of the hole and then went about his business. That, Tom thought, might explain how a ten-foot pike felled a six-foot-six-ish man. What Barbara was doing in Morchard Wood didn't need explaining. He knew women in particular loathed the malodourous portaloos and would—if there were any decent opportunity and they weren't too genteel—risk spending a penny behind a tree in the woods. And despite her anguish at the scene there was, Tom thought from his brief acquaintance with her, a resolute edge to Barbara Coaker. A stolidness.

And yet, Tom considered as he nicked himself with the razor—*Jesus H!*—there was something peculiar about the scene—or perhaps it was Barbara's fraught description—that seemed tantalizingly out of his mind's reach, however much he concentrated. His hand went unthinkingly to a towel on the rack, concentration vanished, bloodying the snowy cotton as he dabbed at his throat. He looked at the mess with dismay. The towels were new. Madrun had bought them only the week before, and she would not be best pleased to find one stained so soon. He tossed it on a chair, reminding himself to remove the stain before it set, when he was done Sunday services, and groped in the cabinet for a sticking plaster.

It was the second time in a month he'd cut himself in the same place, above his Adam's apple. What would his flock think if he grew a beard? They were the vogue again, particularly among young men, and he'd had one part of a year when he'd been studying at the vicar factory in Cambridge. The beard had given him, he'd thought then, a kind of clerical *gravitas*. But he'd been—what?—twenty-six. He was forty now. A beard would likely make him look grizzled. He was starting to notice flecks of grey.

A little later, at the service, during the prayers of intercession, he unthinkingly included Charles Rouse's name and realised as the words passed his lips he should have waited for the following Sunday, after authorities had released it. A kind of gasp sounded from someone in the sanctuary, but was quickly subsumed in the murmurs of "hear our prayer." Tom glanced about for the source, but discerned nothing on the faces of his usual parishioners other than a regrettable sheepishness. Summer worship services sometimes attracted one-offs—holidaymakers seeking the West Country beaches, the occasional American looking for some sort of authentic country church "experience." The latter—often in short trousers and T-shirts—was most likely to fall into gauche behaviour. Perhaps that wasn't a gasp he heard but the shush of an iPhone camera.

But when the service was finished and he was standing at the north porch of the church, chatting with those taking their leave, he noted Roger Pattimore loitering near the ancient yew tree that dominated the churchyard. Roger was in the choir, but he rarely lingered after church as he had to hurry back to the village shop he owned, and to his mother who ailed from most everything under the sun and had been doing so with vigilance since Ted Heath's premiership.

"How's Enid this morning?" Tom called toward Roger conversationally after the last congregant had passed toward the lych-gate.

"Oh, bless, poor Mother, she's lately a martyr to her bowels, as you know," Roger began. "She's certain it's gluten that's giving her gyp."

Tom sighed inwardly. Introducing gluten-free sacramental bread had divided his Parochial Church Council. He was quite happy to offer an alternative, but some PCC members got very heated that the Body of Christ be unblemished by current health trends. "Womanish nonsense!" declared formidable PCC chair Karla Skynner, herself a woman.

"I'm sorry for your mother's suffering," Tom worded his reply for truth's sake. He *was* sorry for the psychological warping of hypochondria. "Anyway...?" he prompted, as he had a few tasks to do in the vestry.

"I thought I heard Charles Rouse's name in the prayers."

"You did."

"Charley Rouse, the coach driver, over Hamlyn way?"

"Was he a coach driver? I didn't know."

"Tall fellow? Really quite tall."

"I would say so, yes," Tom replied, though "long" might be the better description as he had only ever viewed the man as horizontal.

"Then he's alive."

"No, Roger, as the prayer indicated, he's not."

"Sorry, I meant to say, 'he's back.'"

"Well, *was* back," Tom responded, growing more

perplexed. "Mrs. Prowse seemed to suggest he'd been away for some years."

Roger's large ruddy face fell into thought. "Then *he* must have been the fellow found dead at the Battle of Thornford, yes? I heard it on the news this morning. You were there?"

"Giving my blessing," Tom replied dryly.

"Charley loved Civil War reenactments."

"Yesterday's seemed more a reenactment of the Brixton riots."

"Yes, rather. Actually, the English Civil War Society blacklisted the Battle of Thornford years ago."

"You were a reenactor?"

"Briefly, in my youth, before Mother … you know. If you stand for King, the costumes are ever so much smarter than Parliament's." Roger brushed a hand over his bald pate as though imagining a feathered Cavalier cap and sighed. "Well, that's a good thing, then."

"What is?"

"That Charley's …"

"Dead?" Tom frowned, filling in the blank.

"Well, bless … not really … I mean …"

Tom observed a contention of emotions travel Roger's features. First Madrun's abrupt reaction, now this. Since he'd been appointed to the living of Thornford Regis, he'd impressed upon his flock his distaste for gossip and scandal-mongering, though it was true stopping the tide of it was about as likely as stopping the tide at Beachy Head. In this instance, however, he felt he'd like to rescind his remonstrations—*what is going on? What are you all keeping from me?*—but he daren't, lest he be accused of hypocrisy.

"… I mean that Charley was lost and now he's found, to quote—"

"Well, physically at any rate." Tom interrupted, feeling still a little at sea. "The hymn is about forgiveness and redemption."

"Oh, I meant physically," Roger said, adding hastily, "And it will be a good thing for Jago."

"Indeed?"

Roger put his hand to his mouth. "Well, perhaps Sharon more. Actually, better for Sharon, really."

"Who is Sharon?"

"Sharon Pearce."

"Oh, yes, Jago's fancy woman." He smiled, using his housekeeper's expression, which she said in a tone suggesting disapproval of her brother's romantic choice. "But why…?"

"Bless, Tom, Sharon is Charley's wife."

"Oh." The penny dropped. *Goodness! The entanglements!* So Jago's ladyfriend, Sharon, was the wife of Charley, who was the brother of Jago's wife, Maureen, who had herself bolted sometime in the past. It all felt like the snow-globe kinships in *Eastenders*.

"You mean," Tom said after a moment's consideration, "that Sharon would now be, say, free to marry. That would be the good coming out of this tragedy?"

Roger blinked. "Yes. That's it. That's what I meant."

Tom absently fingered the plaster on his neck. "There's something else?"

"No, not really."

Roger's tone was breezy, and Tom wasn't fooled. As Roger turned up the pea shingle toward the lych-gate, he called after him:

"By the way, when I said Charley Rouse's name in the prayers, I thought I heard someone make a sort of noise. It might have been behind me, in the quire. Was that you?"

Roger turned slightly. "Me? No, he replied, dashing through the lych-gate into Church Walk.

3

Monday

Monday was the vicar's day off, and there being no rest for the wicked, in his housekeeper's parlance, Tom—feeling not in the least wicked—was packed off to Morrisons in nearby Totnes with a longish list. Grocery shopping he normally found a bore and a chore, but he parked those feelings in this instance as he had another task in town that he didn't want Madrun to know about. Or anybody really—at least not quite yet.

He was going to sign up for dancing lessons. And he felt a bit silly about it. Before taking training as a priest, he'd been a magician, his hands his bread-and-butter. But whatever natural grace had been afforded his upper extremities had not extended to his lower ones. And there was another reason for taking dancing lessons. But he didn't care to admit that to himself.

He parked at Morrisons, paid at the pay-and-display, but headed off instead for Fore Street and a certain building he knew housed a dance studio. He could simply have signed up for the course online, but he sought a reassuring recce of the space first.

He found the space slightly intimidating. The Ballroom Blitz studio was on the top floor of a structure composed of two eighteenth-century merchant's houses knocked together, but like the TARDIS on *Doctor Who* it was somehow bigger on the inside than it was on the outside. Perhaps the glittering mirrors marshalled around the room gave the effect, he thought, as he stepped through the door and saw his reflection across the room stepping through the door. His eyes spun around the painted panels of dancing graces and nymphs and satyrs and Zeus in his majesty interspaced between the mirrored glass, at the crystal wall sconces, at the velvet drapes, at the red and gold and red and gold and red and gold, gold, gold, up to the gilt ceiling anchoring two elaborate chandeliers and thought he was either going to have to dust off his best dress suit sharpish or reconsider this enterprise, perhaps take a course in conversational Urdu or something.

And then a hand grasped his wrist. It belonged to a women *d'un certain âge*, her hair pulled back in severe chignon, her eyes glittering with some undecipherable emotion. As there was something vaguely eastern European about the interior furnishings, Tom wasn't surprised her English echoed of somewhere east of the Elbe. She led him through the application process.

"Do you get any stick from the people below you?" he asked when he'd finished filling in the form and was handing it back to her.

"Stick?" She regarded him speculatively, her eyes falling to his clerical collar or perhaps to the new plaster stuck on his neck, he wasn't sure.

"I mean, do people below you complain about the noise?" He imagined the thunder of dozens of feet along the wooden floor.

The woman—her name, she said, was Madame Sergeyev—raised a single, rigorously plucked eyebrow and drawled throatily: "I own the building."

Mark Tucker was leaning against the wall at the bottom of the stairwell, his phone in front of his eyes, when Tom descended from the gloom above. He thought if Mark was so glued to the thing, he might slip past unnoticed. But no such luck.

Mark's eyes lifted from his phone, met Tom's, glanced to the stairs.

"Hello, Tom," he said cheerily. "What brings you here. Appointment with Elk?"

"Well, no." Tom couldn't lie. Elkanah Mayhew was part of The Mayhew Group, insurance brokers occupying the first floor. Mark was a solicitor with Tucker, Tucker & Tucker on the ground floor and a churchwarden at St. Nicholas's. "I think I've got all the insurance I need."

Mark's eyes moved again to the stairs, but before he could venture another guess, a door slammed noisily and the stair sounded with treading feet anew. A young man with a full beard emerged from shadow, holding a gym bag.

"Tom's joining us for lunch, Elk," Mark said, glancing at Tom for assent.

"Oh?" Elk sounded faintly surprised, but recovered quickly. "That's grand. You're not coming to spinning class, too, are you?"

"No," Tom laughed. "I like to *get* somewhere when I'm on a bicycle."

At the Waterside Bistro, once they'd received their meals, talk turned to the unpleasantness at the Battle of Thornford as it hadn't yet vanished from the news cycle. The victim had been named.

"Tom was there," Mark said, lifting his glass of sparkling water.

"You weren't at yesterday's service, for one thing." Tom looked up from his cheese and chutney sandwich. ""How do you know?"

"Oh, Tom."

"Sorry." He'd momentarily forgotten that gossip generally blew through Thornford Regis like something disagreeable through a goose.

"Pretty gruesome sight, I expect," Elkanah said.

"It was." Tom's mind returned to the scene: Sunlight filtering through trees, glinting cruelly off the blade torn through Charley Rouse's neck, blood pooling nastily on the forest floor, absent birdsong, almost dead silence. A detail emerged unbidden: Charley's eyes had been closed, as if he were in a dream of peace. But as he had died without warning, oughtn't they to have been open, staring into nothingness? True, closed eyes at death did not necessarily mean composure or restfulness nor open eyes fear or alarm, but totting up his experiences as a priest Tom matched moments of sudden death with open eyes. Or, Tom thought, was he just being fanciful?

"The suggestion from reports seems to be that it was an accident of some kind," Mark flicked a glance at Tom as if seeking confirmation.

Tom shrugged. "I don't know," he responded. Madrun's and Roger's queer reactions gave him pause, but he said nothing. "There'll be an inquiry, of course. There has to be when the death isn't natural. So I expect we'll have to—"

A shriek of shattering glass cut him off.

"—wait," Tom finished his thought, looking toward a nearby server who had dropped a tray and was now suffering the applause of some patrons.

"You know," Elkanah said, lowering his voice as another server rushed forward with a brush, "he had insurance, Charles Rouse."

"But don't most folk have—" Mark began.

"Reenactors' insurance."

Tom and Mark look at each other across the table and said at the same time, "There's reenactors' insurance?"

"There is. Individual or group. Look, these plonkers can do themselves—or others—a serious injury. Pikes, pistols, cannons, guns, black powder, horses. Blokes who like to have-a-go at archery." Elk stroked his beard. "It can cover damage to their kit, travelling back and forth, damage to property—"

"But I gather Charley Rouse hasn't lived in these parts for eight or nine years," Tom interrupted.

"He still paid the premiums every month."

"How?"

"Standing order with a bank."

"Blimey, he must have been mad keen," Mark remarked draining his glass.

"He must have been," Elk agreed. "Policies are rated individually on how frequently you attend such events, so Mr. Rouse's premiums were on the high side."

"Then," Tom asked, "what would be the payout for—?"

"For accidental death at a reenactment? Oh, a little south of a quarter million pounds, I'd estimate."

"'Accidental.'"

"Yes, Vicar. Accidental. If it's demonstrated to be caused otherwise …" Elk raised his eyebrows. "Hence my interest."

"And may I ask who's named the beneficiary of Charley Rouse's policy?"

Elkanah ran his hand through his beard again, and grinned. "You may."

"Well, then, who—"

"You have to keep it to yourselves, mind. It *is* confidential for the time being. I trust you, Vicar. Mark, on the other hand…"

"Are you having a laugh?" Mark slugged Elk's shoulder. "I know when to keep *schtum*. I'm a lawyer."

"All right then." Elkanah named a name.

"Oh," Mark said.

"Not a complete surprise, I guess," Tom added.

Tom was in the condiments aisle at Morrisons, trying to locate a certain Welsh mustard, when his phone went off in his pocket. He had a good idea who the caller was, and he was only a little disappointed that he was right when he saw the name emblazoned on the screen.

"Mr. Christmas," the voice began without preliminaries, "have you had an accident?"

"Not so you'd know," he replied, dipping his head to survey the lower shelves.

"It's gone half two."

"Has it really. Mrs. Prowse, any chance you could do without Welsh mustard. I can't seem to locate it."

"Have you looked at the very bottom shelf?"

"The blood is rushing to my head this very minute."

"You may have to get on your knees."

"I'm wearing my collar, Mrs. Prowse. People will get the wrong idea."

A slight harrumph came down the line. "You have visitors."

"Hence the call?" Tom straightened and felt a twinge along his back.

"I thought you'd be home by one, so when they called I said come at two."

"'They' being...?"

"The local constabulary."

"CID?"

"Yes."

"Bliss or Blessing?"

"And, not or."

"Ah, both barrels. Well, tell them I'll be along shortly. Give them tea. Lard it with your legendary pastries and such."

"I'm not without foresight, Mr. Christmas."

"Good show. Oh, look! There's Welsh mustard on the *top* shelf, of all places!"

"It's got no business being there! Now everyone will be buying it."

"Only tall people, Mrs. Prowse."

On the short drive home to Thornford from Totnes, Tom's mind went walkabout. Of course, one's spouse is most often the beneficiary of an insurance policy. Little startling there. The puzzle was that Charley maintained Sharon as his beneficiary despite an almost decade long estrangement. Which spoke of what? Enduring affection? Guilt? Sheer forgetfulness?

Sharon was Sharon Pearce—Mrs. Charles Rouse in the old style. To Tom, who had been appointed to the living in Thornford Regis less than two years earlier, she was only an occasional presence in the village, spotted at the pub more recently with Jago, for instance, or at Pattimore's, the village shop, though her home—Tom presumed—was in Hamlyn. Elsewise all he knew of her was that she managed Little Stars Childminders, which was located at Thorn Barton farm, but as his daughter, Miranda, at eleven, was past the childminding years, he paid the service little attention. Mark's daughter, Ruby, however, was only three. He and his wife, Violet, were shopping around.

In his glimpsing of Sharon, she appeared to be the sort of woman you might expect to manage a childminding service, vaguely harried, but in good control. He wondered if she had any children of her own, though, he expected, like Jago's daughters, Tamara and Kerra, they'd probably be entering adulthood. Now that he understood the familial connection—the marital and blood ties between the Prowses and the Rouses—it seemed perhaps fitting that romance would blossom between these two well-acquainted people. Perhaps misery does love company. Each had a spouse who'd left the marriage bed.

After Tom turned off the A435 on to the road leading to the village, at the corner where Manor Bend intersected with Pennycross Road, he passed Thorn Cross Garage—or, rather, as its sign proclaimed, TH RN CR SS GARAGE, the 'O's having vanished in the mists of time. He glanced at his fuel gauge: he would have to fill up tomorrow, before he drove to Exeter to fetch his daughter, and this recalled to him an American expression Madrun had used uncharacteristically in passing a few weeks earlier about the garage, which her brother owned, as his father had before him: Jago, she'd said, would have to "go big or go home."

If you're going big, Tom thought unhappily, the Americanism now freighted with new significance, you need money. And had he not glimpsed Jago for a moment at the Battle of Thornford? He had.

He abandoned these thoughts as he pulled into the vicarage. Across Church Lane, next to the Church House Inn, he could see glinting in the sun a familiar red Astra, indicating Detective Inspector Derek Bliss and Detective Sergeant Colin Blessing, Totnes CID, had not abandoned their business in the village. He rather wished they had. He'd engaged with them over other incidents in the parish and hadn't found them always smooth sailing.

Madrun had parked the two men in what she insisted on calling the drawing room, rather than in his untidy study where they'd convened on past occasions. She'd also pulled out the best china, as if she was expecting minor royalty to drop by. Tom glimpsed Bliss and Blessing from an angle before they saw him. Both were fleshy men, with hands like ham hocks and both, he noted, were struggling valiantly to free fat forefingers from finicky teacup handles. On a low table in front of them was the full tea service, a groaning array of tiny sandwiches and cakes. Whatever was she up to, Madrun? Was she trying to keep them sweet? Literally?

"Gentlemen," he greeted them, "Sorry for the delay. I was in town. If I'd known, I could have met you there."

"What were you doing in town?" DI Bliss spoke brusquely, setting his cup down.

"Um ..." Tom felt caught off-guard. He didn't want the world and its mother to know he was taking dancing lessons. "Grocery shopping," he replied, seating himself opposite, noting their frowns, as if it weren't the done thing for a working man to be shopping of a Monday afternoon.

"It's my day off," he explained, wondering why Madrun hadn't supplied a third cup, for him. He smiled and addressed the detective-sergeant: "I understand Mrs.

25

Blessing has been cast in the autumn play at the village hall here. *Neuf Femmes*, I think it's being called. Congratulations."

"None of my doing, Vicar," DS Blessing said in a disinterested tone.

Having learned that small talk was wasted on the pair, Tom got to the point: "I expect you're here because of Charles Rouse's death."

"We are."

"I should probably have stayed longer at the reenactment and given a statement then. I do apologise, but …" It occurred to him he never did see any police presence at the event. "Were no—?"

"A private affair, Vicar," Blessing anticipated him. "On private property. Hailstone Field is part of Lord Fookes's estate. He can hire private security if he wants. Likely bloody should have," he added, scraping his teacup against the saucer. "Foolish not to. Can you take us through the events?"

As Blessing scribbled in a note pad, Tom outlined what he could recall, from his own advance toward the portaloos to Barbara's wraithlike emergence from the woods. "Have you spoken with Barbara Coaker, vicar of—?"

"We have." Bliss said.

"Barbara was in great distress, quite understandably. She sort of gestured toward the wooded area—Morchard Wood—off behind the loos. Given her state, I did as I was bidden, walked a little ways in, and there was … well, you might imagine."

"You got right out again?

"Well, yes, he was obviously—"

"Did Miss Coaker know who he was?" Blessing

asked, looking up from his notebook. Invariably, Blessing, the older man, though junior in rank, asked most of the questions and did all the recording.

"I ... I don't think so. She didn't appear to."

"Did you?"

"No idea. No one seemed to. My doing, probably. I advised people to stay well away, though one of the reen-actors—a Thornfordite, it must have been—identified him to me."

"Thornfordite, why? Because of a floppy hat, yes? Thornford was for the king."

"Yes."

"To identify him, he must have either known or seen Mr. Rouse."

Tom reflected. "I suppose that's true."

"Could you identify this person?"

"Well ..." Tom frowned in thought. "All I can remem-ber is that he was rather short, five-six or -seven? A bit stocky. A kid, really. But the hat, you know. I was looking down on it and from my perspective it blocked most of his face. The feather tickled, too." He searched his thoughts for some other useful details but came up empty. "Other than that, the usual clobber the other Cavaliers were wearing—breeches, tarted-up Wellies, some sort of leather gloves. Sorry."

"Voice? Accent?"

"Local, I'd say." He watched Bliss reach for one of Madrun's famous—sometimes infamous—yewberry tarts. "Why? *Are* you thinking Rouse's death is not accidental?"

Bliss shrugged as he popped the tart in his mouth. Blessing replied, "This is what we're trying to determine."

Tom lurched suddenly. One of the vicarage cats, either Powell or Gloria (almost indistinguishable but for the tuckings in their backsides), manifested on his lap and stretched toward the milk jug.

"No!" Tom restrained the animal. "Then … might you have a motive, if it's not accidental?"

"Mr. Christmas, as you know—"

"Sorry, Detective-Inspector. I know. You can't say."

Bliss shifted in his chair. "And then after—?"

"After? I went back to the St. John's Ambulance tent, to look in on Barbara, and then came home."

"Have you spoken with Miss Coaker since?"

"No, but I'm seeing her tomorrow at the deanery dine and whine."

"The …?"

"It's a monthly church meeting."

The two men's eyes seemed to glaze over. Blessing asked, "You're certain you yourself didn't know Charles Rouse?"

Tom frowned at the repeated question. "Not at all, Detective-Sergeant. As you know, I've only lived in Thornford a short time, so … oh, thank you," he said to Madrun who had stepped in at that moment and handed him a mug (*a mug?*) for his tea.

"I'll just remove Gloria," she said, collecting the cat.

"Mrs. Prowse knew Rouse, though," Tom continued, reaching for the milk jug. "She's lived here most of her life," he added unnecessarily. "Mrs. Prowse?"

"I can't say I knew him at all." Madrun's tone was dismissive.

Tom glanced up sharply from the jug, nearly spilling the milk on his lap. Madrun's expression, as she turned, was severe and her words felt like a warning. He shifted his eyes to the detectives, who were regarding them curiously. Tom gave them a thin smile. "I must have got the wrong end of the stick," he said, reaching for the teapot as Madrun exited the room. "I did hear … somewhere … that Mr. Rouse had been absent from these parts for many years."

"That's our understanding," Bliss said.

"Had he been back long?"

"Perhaps a month," Blessing added, licking a finger and turning a page in his notebook.

"Where had he been living?" Tom poured tea into his mug.

"I think we're the ones supposed to be asking the questions, Vicar." Blessing looked up.

Tom sighed. "I merely thought, Detective-Sergeant, that if he'd left behind loved ones somewhere, I might pay a pastoral visit."

Blessing glanced at his senior partner who signalled assent. "He was living at a caravan park outside Hamlyn, with a woman and her daughter. East European of some nature."

"Do you have a name by chance?" he asked, stirring his tea.

"Name of what?"

"Park or woman."

"By chance, no." It was Bliss's turn to reply and it was curt, as was Bliss's habit. "Another question, Vicar: did you happen to see anyone else you know at the reenactment? Anyone who might have known Mr. Rouse?"

Tom kept his eyes on the milky cloud of tea before him and let a hearty sip mask his hesitation. "No," he said.

He very much disliked fibbing.

After seeing the detectives out, Tom went through to the kitchen, mug in hand.

"That," he said to Madrun as he took the last cress and cucumber sandwich off the tray, "was a bit of a posh tea for a Monday afternoon."

"They looked like they needed bucking up."

"They look like they could each lose two stone," Tom rejoindered, adding darkly, "I don't think you can curry favour with scones and a few bitty sandwiches, Mrs. Prowse."

"As you happen on curry, Mr. Christmas," Madrun turned to the sink, "shall I do you a tikka masala for your supper?"

One of Tom's tiny regrets of village life was that he couldn't just pop down the road for a takeaway curry the way he could in Bristol or London or Gravesend where he'd lived before. He knew Madrun was buttering him up for some reason, but he replied, humbly, "that would be lovely." A change from Monday's usual cold roast.

"Mrs. Prowse," he added, after a moment's hesitation, "why did you tell the detectives that you didn't know Charley Rouse?"

"I said I couldn't say I knew him."

"You couldn't say or wouldn't say?"

"I would say if I could say."

"But you can say, can you not?"

"No, I can't say."

Tom took a breath. "I think you mean something along the lines of no one really knows everything about another person."

Madrun paused in her handwashing of the good china. "I could say that."

"This doesn't have anything to do with Jago, does it?"

"That I can't say."

"I think," Tom said with a sigh. "I'm going to have a lie-down."

30

4

Tuesday

Tom watched the numbers tick up on the pump display with the customary dismay. Petrol was among life's necessities, but one he quietly begrudged paying for, much as he did car repairs. Sixty-five pounds might better be spent on new school clothes for Miranda. He wondered sometimes if Jago—for it was Jago manning the pump—was at all troubled by undertones of resentment from customers or were his defences solid. Certainly he looked discomfited this morning.

Tom bit his lip and said, "I'm sorry for your recent loss. Madrun told—"

"If you mean Charley Rouse, Vicar, you can save your breath to cool your porridge."

"Ah, well, your sister seemed to indicate there was no love lost."

"That's an understatement." Jago flicked him a sharp glance. "If you think I had anything to do with—"

"I don't think it's been determined—"

"Madrun tells me the coppers paid you a visit yesterday."

"I happened to be at the reenactment Saturday. Have

31

they spoken with you?"

"The cops? Why would they speak to me?"

Tom shrugged. "Family connection? And you were there."

"I was where?"

"At the Battle."

Jago glowered. "It was a service call. I don't have any interest in that reenactment bollocks."

"Tow?" Tom glanced at the truck parked in the yard.

"In the end. Car wouldn't start. Needed a new ignition switch." Jago replaced the nozzle in its cradle.

Tom followed his burly figure inside the garage, reaching absently into his pocket for his wallet, his mind's eye on the scene at the Battle of Thornford. Jago, he was certain, had been at the front of the spectators for a time. A moment's respite from car servicing? Curiosity? Or …?

Inside, Jago took his credit card and stuffed it into the card reader.

"How is business by the way?" Tom asked lightly as he punched in his pin code. He looked up to see Jago regarding him speculatively.

"Fine. Why? Has my sister been nattering about something?"

"Well …"

Jago scowled. "Then not so bloody fine. These are not best days for independent garages, Tom. Trained help hard to find, taxes, financing tighter than a crab's arse. Do you know I get less than a penny on a litre of gas? It's either the end of the line for this place that my grandfather built or I—"

"Go big," Tom supplied.

"Something like that, but mustn't grumble as Madrun would say." Jago handed back the credit card and watched as Tom returned it to his wallet. "So, where are you off to?" he asked as if eager to change the subject.

"Torbay Hospital first. I'm fine," he added when Jago shot him a concerned glance. "Pastoral visits. Jeanette Neels, for one."

"I heard. Hip replacement. How is she?"

"On the mend," Tom replied hopefully. Jeanette was the matriarch of the eight women who collectively owned and operated Thorn Barton, a nearby dairy farm and farm shop. But her life was complicated by multiple sclerosis. "And then I'm going up to Exeter to collect my daughter. She's had a few days in France with her aunt."

"And school starts again next week."

"It does." Tom eyes travelled to a certain red object on a shelf behind Jago's head. "Is that Madrun's?"

"It is."

"That's why I haven't heard the usual pounding away lately."

Madrun wrote a daily letter to her deaf mother in Cornwall, on a typewriter, of all quaint objects.

"Problem with the 'e' key," Jago explained. "I don't know how long I can go on fixing her typewriter. It's the twenty-first century! I expect Maddy's going spare without the thing."

"Your mother must wonder what's happened."

"There are other ways to keep in touch with my mother, but you know what my sister's like."

"I've offered to buy her a nice little laptop and show her how to use it."

"Best of luck with that." Jago gave him a flinty smile. "Tell her I'll have it for her Thursday. I'll drop it off on the way to the pub quiz."

An open copy of the *Western Morning News* rose and fell gently over Jeanette's chest, its edge, tucked to her chin, rippling to her even breaths. The banner story was about a hotel fire in Plymouth, but Tom's eye went to a squib about Charley Rouse's death in the bottom right corner. Its subhead invited readers to an inside page for a feature on the dangers of reenactments—one of those tut-tut-we-told-you-so follow-ups newspapers liked to do, which suggested that Rouse's death, at least in some quarters, was still being regarded as accidental.

He wondered if he should simply leave Jeanette be. Having landed at hospital himself, as a teenager, to have his appendix removed, he knew a decent sleep was lost to the thrum and rattle and squeak of a ward at night. The room, semi-private (the other bed was occupied by a champion snorer), was stuffy, and the August weather wasn't to blame. A heater was mindlessly churning away somewhere and the windows, typically for hospitals, were sealed shut, as if the theory that night air caused disease remained current.

But as he was about to turn for the door, Jeanette stirred, her eyes blinking open, taking in the room—and Tom—as though exiting a dream.

"Tom," she greeted him, shifting slightly and wincing.

"Pain?"

"Some. But I have this jolly little button to press." She reached for the PCA pump by her side. "Of course, the drug sends me off to the land of Nod half the time." She sighed and looked down past the newspaper to the hip spica peeking out from beneath the sheets. "It will be good to be back home." She beckoned Tom closer and whispered, "When my roommate isn't snoring like a hyena, she's barking orders to her husband, who, I'm led to believe, is dead."

"She's quiet now."

"You just wait." She lifted the paper from her chest with tremoring hands and folded it. "I was reading about this death at that ridiculous reenactment. The council should have put a stop to it years ago, or else turned it into something that doesn't frighten the horses, not to mention the women and children."

"I was there."

"You were?"

"To give Communion. Along with Barbara Coaker, from All Saints. Do you know—?"

"Oh, Barbara. Of course, I know her. I'd forgotten she'd returned. When she was a teenager, she worked in the farm shop for a few summers. Odd duck, she was. No, that's unkind. She had her struggles." She smiled at Tom. "She's done well. Had a wretched home life, I think. Mother died very young and her father was a bit of a waster. Trawlerman out of Brixton. If he wasn't out to sea he was down the pub. Barbara had to be mother to her little sister. Sorry, Tom, you must know all this."

"I don't, really. Barbara's only had the living at Hamlyn a few months. At deanery meetings we're more preoccupied with church business." He gestured to the newspaper. "It was Barbara, in fact, who came across Charley Rouse, the man who died."

"Oh … good heavens." Jeanette's eyes twitched in their sockets, an effect of the MS, but her voice held, Tom thought, a curiously pensive tone. "Poor woman. Is she all right?"

"Well, shattered at the time, of course, but—I'm not sure …" He had a guilty thought: I should have given her a call. "I'll be seeing her this evening at our monthly meeting. And then she'll be at the pub quiz fundraiser later this week. I—" A loud snort from behind the dividing curtain interrupted him. "I hope she's better."

"The Coakers lived over the road from the Rouses for years," Jeanette said, her eyes following Tom's to the curtain.

"Really? How odd. Barbara never said, but of course she was in shock."

"It was Sharon Rouse who suggested Barbara for the farm shop," Jeanette continued. "You know Sharon—Sharon Pearce now. She operates Little Stars at the farm. She'd just started the service around then, when was this—a dozen years ago? Maybe more. A year or two before Charley upped sticks at any rate."

"Do you know why the marriage ended?"

Jeanette was opening her mouth to reply when the patient in the next bed suddenly barked, "Herbert!"

"That's the dead husband," Jeannette whispered. "Anyway, what were we—?"

"The Rouses' marriage."

"Oh," Jeanette's eyes darted to the curtain again as if it were a barrier to further conversation. "I don't really know. Sharon never quite said. She's so very good at what she does. Lovely with the little ones."

Tom frowned, feeling he was being fobbed off somehow. Jeanette bit her lip, as if in indecision. After a moment, she said, "He came up to the farm, Charley."

"You mean, back in—"

"No. Last week, before I came here for surgery. Funny to see him after so long. He looked worse for wear. I think folk thought for years he might be dead."

"What did he have to say?"

"He didn't speak with me. He spoke with Sharon. I

could see them near the old ash house. Arguing, it looked like." A look of horror crossed her weathered face. "Not that that means anything, Tom. I wouldn't want to get Sharon in bother. I'm sure it was nothing important."

Tom could see the worry and the lie in Jeanette's eyes. A man doesn't manifest himself after a near decade's absence to have a barney with his wife over who lost the car keys. "I'm sure," he agreed reassuringly as he began unpacking his portable Communion set and the woman in the next bed sawed wood into a fine grind.

"Bonjour, Papa."

"Bonjour, ma petite patate," Tom replied, bending on the hall rug to give his daughter a hug.

"Potato, Daddy? Really?"

"I'm running out of fruit and veg I know in French. *Ma petite asperge?*

"That's a little more elegant, Tom," his sister-in-law Julia remarked dryly, her arms folded over a striped apron. She was standing behind Miranda, a wooden spoon in hand.

"And like *asperges* you seem to have shot up since I saw you last. Whatever have you been eating in Paris?"

"Pastries," Julia replied.

"Better than Mrs. Prowse's?" Tom addressed his daughter.

"Different," Miranda replied after a pause.

"A fine answer. Best you say that to Mrs. Prowse."

"How *are* things in Glocca Morra?" Julia led Tom deeper into her apartment, toward her kitchen as Miranda veered toward the bedrooms. Tom savoured Julia's ironic tone, as he savoured the luscious aromas in the kitchen. If Thornford Regis had seemed—at least at first—a haven

37

of peace for him after the cruel death of his wife, Lisbeth, in Bristol, the village had been less so for Julia, who had fled in the wake of a broken marriage. In Exeter, she had resumed her maiden name—Rose—and reestablished her career as a music teacher, at the Bramdean School.

"The usual mayhem," Tom replied lightly, never sure if Julia had any real appetite for news of her former home. He sat down on a stool and touched on a few benign matters: actress Cat Northmore's buzzworthy return to the village, preparations for the autumn amateur theatrical; asked a few questions about their trip to France after he'd left them in London, but added, with a little reluctance:

"There was a spot of unpleasantness at the weekend though."

"Oh?" Julia bent to peek into the oven.

"A man died at the Battle of Thornford reenactment."

"You were there? Tom, what on earth were you doing at that awful thing?"

"Blessing it, more or less. They asked, and I came. I'd give such an invitation a hard think next time, though. I'm not sure about blessing armies going into battle, even if it's a mock battle. Have you ever been?"

"Oh, Tom, don't be ridiculous."

Tom laughed. Sometimes Julia so reminded him of Lisbeth, the way she could be delightfully demolishing. "There *were* women there."

"Long-suffering wives or girlfriends, I presume. Can you name a female equivalent of such nonsense?"

Tom considered the question as Julia handed him a glass of wine. "Don't women dress up as Jane Austen and congregate at the Pump Room in Bath?"

"They don't go about having a bash at each other over

cucumber sandwiches."

"*Vive la différence*, I suppose. And, in fact, most of the women more or less absented themselves as the battle, so-called, was about to begin."

"I'd always understood it had descended into little more than a public brawl."

"I'm loath to admit it, but I did experience a strange sort of animal thrill for a bit. Even," he mused, sipping the wine, a crisp *pinot gris*, "Barbara seemed caught up in it."

"Barbara?"

"Sorry. Coaker, the new vicar of All Saints. In Hamlyn. She blessed the Roundhead side."

"Barbara Coaker. I remember her. So, she went into the church."

"And pitched up at home, basically," Tom reflected. "But surely she was gone to uni before you started teaching at Hamlyn Grammar."

"She was. But she more or less stood *in loco parentis* for her sister Elise, would attend sports days and prize-giving and the like. There was a fair age gap between the two. I forget the details. Mother died young, I think, father not up to much."

"I've heard that."

"She was an unusual girl, Elise. Extremely bright. Aced her GCSEs. Music and English weren't her forte but she was a star in the sciences and maths. Quirky, though. Struggled socially, poor thing. You know what teenagers can be like. There may have been other problems, but I wasn't the school counselor. I do remember the sensation she caused when she came to school one day having traded her long hair for a rather fierce buzz cut."

"Tomboy?"

"There's a quaint word." Julia removed a quiche from

the oven. "Possibly struggling with her sexuality in some fashion, I expect. I'm not sure what became of her. I don't think she attended the sixth form school."

"Daddy?" Miranda voice sounded behind him. Tom turned in his seat.

"Paris?" he asked, startled by the sophistication of the dress his daughter was now wearing. Miranda nodded. It was midnight blue, of some sort of opulent fabric, with a fitted top section and a skirt that flared out to knee length. He felt a pang, wishing Lisbeth were here to share this, to approve or disapprove, though surely Julia approved. Suddenly, Miranda seemed the essence of budding womanhood. She'd put her hair up, too, he noted, before looked down to meet her dark eyes, which sought his approval.

"Stunning," he said, putting into his voice the full force of an enthusiasm he wasn't sure he felt.

Miranda grinned and did a twirl. Julia went over and adjusted a strap. "She's growing up, Tom."

"I can see that. Well, we'll have to have a party just for the frock." He cleared the frog from his throat. "How about the new uniform and such?" Miranda had burst out of her old one, and next year, he thought, with a new pang, she would leave the village primary for the big school in Hamlyn.

"Thomas Moore's had most everything," Julia replied. "Miranda?"

"I need a new pencil case and some notebooks and … I have the list."

"Let's stop at the Asda in Newton Abbot," Tom suggested. "I'm sure the back-to-school section is in full bloom. Heaven knows they've probably got the Halloween displays up."

"I'll change back," Miranda said turning, brushing her skirt back with a deftly adult gesture.

Julia was studying his face. "You're all right with this? I know it's a little sophisticated, but …"

"I trust your judgment, Julia. Women's fashion isn't my bailiwick and I don't think Mrs. Prowse is versed in fashion tips for preteen girls." He swirled the wine in his glass and sighed. "It seems like only last month Miranda was in short trousers and T-shirt crabbing with the Swan kids at the millpond. Now she's going to the ball.

"She was more the tomboy type, I thought, before," he added.

"Which reminds me," Julia pulled a prepared salad from the fridge. "You didn't say who died at the reenactment."

"Yes, sorry. It was a man named Charles Rouse— Charley Rouse."

"Oh."

"Familiar?"

Julia reflected. "Isn't he … wasn't he Maureen Prowse's brother? Jago's brother-in-law? A driver—"

"Yes."

"—for Cooper's Coaches. We hired them for school outings."

"Then you'd met him."

"Well … I don't recall him driving us anywhere, at least when I was taking the kids around. Let me think." Julia pulled bottles of oil and vinegar from a cupboard. "I remember: he'd sometimes fetch Elise from school—"

"What? In the coach?"

"No, Tom." She shot him an amused glance as she measured dried mustard into a cruet. "If there was some after-hours sports meet or the like and the school bus had

41

gone, he was one of those on a list who could pick her up. Her father didn't often show. I remember waiting with Elise once or twice for either of them to arrive and, of course, it wasn't her father. Charley was mostly memorable because he was quite tall."

"He didn't he impress you in any other way, did he?"

"Not that I can think." She looked up from the cruet. "Why?"

Tom shrugged. "It's the manner of his death."

"I was going to ask. He can't have been that old."

"Forty-seven, according to the reports."

"Reports?"

"You would have missed the story while you were in Paris. Charley died in a rather freakish manner."

"How?"

"I shall tell you."

"Daddy," Miranda began in a tone recognisable as Tom pulled into the Asda car park and switched off the ignition. "What were you talking about with Aunt Julia earlier."

"When?"

"When I was changing clothes."

"Oh. Well, nothing very important. Nothing for you to worry about." He glanced at her as he fiddled with the buckle on his seat belt and saw doubt in her eyes. "Really, darling, it's—"

"I think that man was killed, don't you?"

Tom felt the loosened seat belt whizz past his shoulder. "So you were listening."

"A little."

Tom stared though the windscreen toward the unlovely slab of the Asda superstore. A sturdy young woman in a green gilet, head to the task, heaved into view pushing a train of empty trolleys across the lot. She rammed the train into the trolley shelter with such sudden force the metallic clang made Tom flinch. He noted her satisfied smile, and the thought flitted through his head that he'd seen her somewhere before, something about her body language—though it may well have been here at Asda as, much as he disliked abandoning the high street shops in Totnes and Torquay, superstore bargains were something even Jesus might find tempting.

"It really is nothing for you to worry about," he repeated.

"I'm not worried, Daddy," she said stoutly. "I'm interested."

It was Tom who was worried. Miranda had lost her mother to a stabbing death in Bristol four years earlier, a murder that remained unsolved. And though Tom moved to a sleepy Devon village in hope of establishing the two of them in a haven of peace, that hope had proven ephemeral. And yet Miranda seemed to have taken several shocking events in her stride, as if her mother's death had somehow steeled her in ways unknown to most other children.

"Then you must have heard enough to come to your conclusion that the man was killed."

"Don't you think so, Daddy?"

Tom bit his lip. "Everyone I've talked with," he said after a moment, "seems quite beholden to the notion that Charley Rouse's death could be nothing more than a ... a bizarre accident."

He had almost said *unfortunate* accident, but hovering over all this was a feeling that Rouse's demise hadn't been entirely unwelcomed, whatever its cause.

"Even the police?"

"I'm not sure what their views are. They don't give

43

·much away, as usual." The car was getting warm; he opened the door to let in a little air. "Why do you think his death wasn't accidental, darling?"

"From something we learned in science."

"And what is that?"

"That badgers dig deep holes, but the holes never go *straight* down."

Deanery meetings, Tom thought sometimes, had more the air of a Christmas party than a business meeting. Eating, drinking and socialising soon swept more serious matters to some corner of twhatever pub they happened to be in. (And they always met in a pub—or an inn or a restaurant.) Difficult issues were rarely addressed and serious, open theological discussion had about as much chance at a deanery as Rochdale had winning the FA Cup Final. And, Tom considered as he lifted a pint of Vicar's Ruin, the fact he'd made a link in his mind to the masculine preserve of football only underscored another fact: despite decades of female ordination, the C of E was still in good measure a man's world, or at least it remained so in this rural back-of-beyond. Barbara Coaker, besides being the newest and youngest member, just happened to be its only woman. And, quaintly, the only one of them wearing a cassock instead of "clericals."

And she didn't appear to be entirely at ease. Small wonder. The sight of Hugh Beeson, vicar of St. Barnabas in Noze Lydiard, all seventeen stone of him kitted out in motorcycle leathers and arriving on his thunderous "Holy Hog," might send a flutter through the hearts of some women, but not Barbara whose smile on greeting travelled nowhere near her eyes. The other men seemed to fall into conversational knots of their own, as they all knew each other, trading stories of who was climbing the greasy pole and who was slipping precipitously down. A certain number of Rabelaisian jokes made the rounds, but voices dropped at the punchline whenever Barbara drew near. It was as if she'd brought her harp to a party and nobody asked her to play.

Afterwards, after administrative matters were got out of the way, after the ever-present worry about church finances was chewed over, and coffee was substituted for ale, Tom drew Barbara aside to ask after her well-being and apologise for not enquiring earlier. Indeed, he apologised on behalf of the other men in the room as it was evident none of them seemed aware of her recent tribulation.

"But then none of the press reports mentioned my name, Tom," she pointed out. "Which is a blessing," she added.

"Still, a horrible happenstance."

"You were there as well."

"But I was forewarned, at least. By you as it happened," he added with a smile she didn't match. Or couldn't. Or wouldn't. She'd struck him before as someone with a humour shortfall and now her eyes—which were either too small or her spectacles too big—rested on him with a deadpan seriousness. He wondered how her congregation warmed to her. "I expect you've had a visit from Totnes CID."

"Oh, yes."

"They're a pair, Bliss and Blessing."

"A pair of what?" Barbara blinked.

"A pair of … detectives," he said lamely. *A pair of tights. A pair of gloves. A pair of scissors.* "I had a visit, too. I couldn't be much help."

"Nor I, I'm afraid. It was all so sudden."

"What was?"

"Coming across ... the body. I couldn't quite take it in at first.

"I know a little of the sensation. My wife—"

"Of course. I had heard. In Bristol ..."

"Lisbeth died in somewhat the same manner." He recalled the shock of finding his wife dead in a pool of her own blood in the very church of which he was priest. "Of course, terrible if the victim is a loved one, but still distressing if you know the victim."

Barbara's furrowed brow delivered a question.

"Charley Rouse," Tom continued. "Wasn't he a neighbour when you were growing up in Hamlyn?"

"Yes." She looked over Tom's shoulder into the depths of pub. "But I didn't know that on Saturday when ... all I saw was the ..." Her mouth formed a grim line. Her eyes returned to Tom's. "Those costumes lend anonymity, wouldn't you say?"

"Yes, I suppose they do." Tom sipped his coffee. "I must say, I found the whole event not quite what I'd expected. I'm a little sorry I gave it a blessing, especially in the light of what happened." He paused for another sip. "Will you be taking the funeral then? Rouses, I presume, have been matched and dispatched at All Saints through the years."

"I don't know." Barbara shifted on her chair. "I've not been approached."

"I gather he was living with a woman and her child at some nearby caravan park. Eastern European of some nature, according to DS Blessing."

"I've no idea."

"Of course, there's Sharon Pearce, to whom I gather Charley is ... was, rather, married." He had the sensation he was talking to himself. "Do you see Sharon? I expect

46

she's not a churchgoer, but I would guess she's still living in the cottage over the road from—"

"She is," Barbara interrupted. "But ours was sold some time ago."

"I thought perhaps your sister might be still ... my sister-in-law mentioned her to me earlier today," he explained. "Julia Rose ... well, you might remember her as Julia Hennis, the music mistress at Hamlyn Grammar—"

"Yes, vaguely. She came on when I was in my last year."

"She remembers your sister as an academic star. Didn't pass on to the sixth form school, though, which seems a pity."

A cloud passed over Barbara's face. "It was a difficult time. Our father died ... for one thing. The house had to be sold. Though that did afford me my education," she added.

"And Elise? Your sister?"

Barbara lowered her eyes. "Following her own path."

"Oh. Well, I hope she's happy in whatever she's doing."

"Anyway, Tom, I must be off."

"I was going to say earlier that I might be able to get the woman's name or address from Bliss or Blessing." Not that I had much luck earlier, he thought.

"What woman?"

"The eastern European one."

"Whatever for?" Barbara slid off her chair.

"I thought, well, you might want to pay her a pastoral visit."

Barbara frowned. "Perhaps, in the circumstances ..."

"I understand." Tom felt a wave of pity for her. "I'll substitute, if you'll allow. I'm more than happy to do so.

See you at the pub quiz Thursday," he called after her, watching her stiff movements in the cassock.

5

Wednesday

Of course, after weeks of glorious sun, it would rain the very day of the coach tour. Tom tilted his umbrella, glanced at the coach in which the driver was affixing a sign reading TINTAGEL to the windscreen, then at the handful of rain-hatted and umbrella'd congregated in front of the village hall. Dismay at the miserably few numbers (this was a fundraiser after all) was relieved when Florence Daintry bellowed: "Everyone's inside, Vicar. You're sinfully *late!*"

Tom wasn't sure he counted five minutes past due as sinful, but he'd learned in his time in Thornford that remonstrating with Florence, bossy-boots of this parish, (well, one of them) was an exercise in futility.

"I'm sure the driver can make up time," he said humbly and was pleased when the driver leaned out of the cab with a thumbs-up and a cheery, "Too right, Vicar!"

His lateness, such as it was, was due to a brief telephone tussle at the vicarage with DI Bliss who refused to disclose contact information for the woman Charley Rouse had been living with before he died.

"But, as I say, I simply want to pay her a kindly visit," he'd repeated.

"That's as maybe, Mr. Christmas," Bliss had countered, impatience crackling down the line, "but we're bound by data protection laws."

"Might I have her name at least?"

"No."

"Why not?"

"This is an ongoing investigation."

"Is it? I thought—"

"Loose ends, Vicar, loose ends."

"I see," Tom said, preparing to drop the receiver in its cradle. "Well, I leave you kindly with this loose end— badger hole! Have a splendid day, Detective-Inspector."

Tom counted the people—mostly women, mostly pensioners—decanting the village hall and scrambling aboard the coach. The good news was that the numbers were made up and some small sum could be added to the church roof fund. Boarding last, rather hoping for a single seat for some quiet contemplation, he couldn't not respond to Venice Daintry's *yoo-hoo* and ended up her seatmate near the front of the vehicle.

"Not sitting with Florence?" he asked conversationally as the coach pulled out of the village.

"We're not joined at the hip, Tom," Venice murmured.

Venice and Florence were not sisters, but sisters-*in-law* who lived together in uneasy juxtaposition, rather like belligerents in the Lombardy Wars. Tom suspected their morning had got off to a poor start with something like: who left toast crumbs in the butter.

"Have you been to Tintagel before?" he asked. He suspected most on the coach had, and were more looking forward to the nosh than to the history. They would be lunching at the St. Kew Inn in Bodmin, with a cream tea later at Jamaica Inn on Bodmin Moor.

"No," Venice replied.

"Really?"

"When you live near a place you always think you'll get there one day. Florence lived in London all her working life and never once visited the Tower."

Tom reflected that he'd lived in Bristol for many years as part of a team ministry at St. Dunstan's, but had never once visited Blaise Castle, one of the city's chief attractions. Nor had he been to Tintagel, where King Arthur was said to dwell.

"Well, I'm looking forward to it," he said, but Venice was now slumped in her seat. He glanced at her, noted with a little sadness—and some understanding—the parchment lids descended over her eyes. There was something soporific about a big coach gliding smoothly on big rubber tires down the carriageway. Perhaps he would nod off himself.

And perhaps he did, for at his next conscious moment he was glimpsing the narrower road northeast of Dartmoor, near Chagford, and Venice, sipping from a hip flask. A *hip flask*. He smelled the sickly aroma of sweet sherry.

"Venice?"

"Oh! I thought you were asleep," she gasped, hastening to turn the flask's screw top. She glanced at him red-faced.

"Are you well?"

"I'm fine." But her tone was strained. She's not fine, Tom considered. Though loath to rush to judgment, sherry at nine-thirty in the morning seemed a little over the top.

"If you're sure …"

51

Venice eased the flask back into her bag. "It's Florence," she said in a low voice. "She really does get on my wick."

"Dare I ask what it is?" *This time?*

"I hired a cleaning lady, you see—"

"Yes?"

"—and she found out."

Tom scratched his head. "But—"

"Florence doesn't believe in cleaning ladies."

"Well, such belief might be thought idolatrous, Venice."

She cast him a withering glance. "Florence is adamantly against them."

"Good heavens, why? You're both—"

"At the far end of life's conveyor belt? Getting down to scrub the tub with my knees is not a treat, Tom, if it ever was. Florence thinks they snoop—cleaning ladies, that is."

"Do they?" he teased.

"Well, of course they don't, if they're worth their salt. They might happen to glance at something now and then, inadvertently, but really! We're two old ladies tucked away in a little West Country village. We're hardly possessed of state secrets."

"Ah," Tom said, "I'm beginning to understand." Before retirement, Florence Dainty had worked for what she called *the ministry*, though what ministry remained ever elusive, as she didn't elucidate and no one dared ask. MI5, Tom wondered at times. MI6? HM Revenue and Customs? The Scottish Office? The Ministry of Agriculture, Fisheries and Food? Who knew? Its legacy, however, was a Florence Daintry with an uncommon streak of vigilance.

"And it didn't help that Florence thought the women I hired was Russian," Venice continued. "'The Cold War is over,' I said to her. 'A leopard doesn't change its spots,' she retorted. Poor Dania. She left in tears yesterday when Florence returned unexpectedly."

Tom frowned.

"You see," Venice continued, lowering her voice once again. "I'd hired her to come Tuesday afternoons. That's when Florence has her regular appointment with the chiropractor in Torquay. And I thought none of the neighbours would notice because Dania doesn't work for one of those services with pink cars that say 'Devon Maids' or the like. She comes on her own in an ordinary car, and I asked her not to bring along cleaning equipment, because we have all of it already. So I thought I could simply pass off her work as my own, you see. And I did quite well, thank you, until Florence got home early because her appointment was cancelled and caught us in the act."

"In the act?"

"Of flipping the mattresses, which is very hard if you don't have someone young around. And Dania was just about to tell me what was upsetting her so terribly."

"So Florence didn't make her cry.

"Florence certainly sent her over the cliff edge." Venice sighed. "It's *my* home, as you know. Florence lives with me. By my leave. Not the other way around."

"Would you like me to have a word?"

"That's very kind, Tom. I'll sort it. Perhaps Florence would tolerate a … Portuguese cleaner. We've been allied with Portugal longer than any other country. They can hardly be after stealing our … recipe for clotted cream. And Dania is Polish, not Russian!" she hissed. "We fought *for* Poland in the last war. Really, Florence is too much."

"Polish," Tom repeated, the nationality tickling his brain. "Where did you find her, this Dania?"

"A little card in the post office window advertising her services caught my eye. I'd been cleaning the kitchen cupboards that day—without Florence's help, mind—and thought, this would be the ticket!"

"No, what I meant was, where does she live?"

"Oh, let me think. Buttles, I think it's called. Buttles Caravan Park."

He knew the place, a small, ill-serviced park surely shunned by the *AA Caravan and Camping Guide* and related websites. Living there suggested a provisional life.

"Do you have her last name?" he asked.

"Oh, dear. I don't think I can pronounce it."

"Do you have it written down? A phone number, perhaps?"

Venice turned to regard him, a kind of wonder on her face. "Has something happened to Madrun?"

"She remains as formidable as ever. No, I have another reason."

"What is it then?"

"Walk with me at Tintagel and I'll tell you. But, Venice, you must promise to keep what I say to yourself. And I mean it."

Fortunately, the clouds began to lift as the coach pulled out of Bodmin, where they visited St. Petroc's Church, and dissolved to a wisp by the time they passed on to the bleak expanse that was Bodmin Moor and the chimneys of Jamaica Inn came into view. Tom had been to the inn once previously—stayed at it, in fact, with Lisbeth, in the early days of their marriage, before Miranda was born, when they had managed to slip away for a minibreak. In stolen moments from a busy medical practice, Lisbeth had been working her way through Daphne du Maurier's Cornwall novels, *Rebecca*, *My Cousin Rachel*, and *Jamaica Inn*, so the destination had all the air of inevitability. It had been early June then, and the gorse on the moor vivid yellow amid the rolling heaths of bracken and heather. They had languished in bed and taken solitary walks and hired a pair of horses and almost got lost. They had rather hoped one of Jamaica Inn's fabled resident ghosts would manifest itself, then hoped that one wouldn't. (None did.)

Then, that is. But one lingered now for Tom, and it was moments such as these, when he glanced into the restaurant where he and she had enjoyed the mixed grill and a bottle of red that he felt Lisbeth's absence most keenly—the way she tossed her head back, laughing her infectious laugh. He could almost see her there, right there, next to the great stone fireplace.

"A penny for 'em, Vicar," said the coach driver, Kevin (according to his name tag), stepping around Tom on his way to the gents'.

"I was recalling another time I spent here. I expect you've been here more than once."

"Lost count."

Tom walked back to exit to the inn's cobbled front yard, its grey stone warmed by flashes of sun. The welcome heat, after a mizzly day at Tintagel and Bodmin, had drawn his charges to take their tea at the outdoor tables. He noticed Venice seated with some of her WI friends (though not with Florence, who was holding court at another table), laughter suggesting her mood of the morning had lightened. She caught Tom's eye and cast him a knowing smile, looking at little like the cat who had caught a canary.

Tom had been surprised Venice had not heard of—or at least couldn't remember seeing or meeting—Charley

Rouse, but then he recalled an old quarrel between the Daintreys and the Prowses that often sent gossip flowing in separate directions. Not knowing Charley explained her obliviousness to the news reports of his death, but that death, Venice was certain, explained Dania's emotional state the day she came to clean.

"But why else would she have been so upset, Tom?" she'd asked as he typed the contact details of Dania Bloczynski (for that was her full name) into his phone.

"You'd think she'd have called to cancel," Tom said as they walked Tintagel's ruins.

"Perhaps she found solace in work," Venice said. "I know I did when my husband died."

"I did, too," Tom had reflected, "when Lisbeth died."

The coach driver approaching, reading something on his phone with frowning intensity, took Tom from his reverie. "Penny for yours?" he asked.

"Just a bit of bother at home. Nothing to worry about." His frown shifted to a broad smile moving Tom to reflect how, in the decades being driven by coach drivers and school bus drivers and train drivers, he gave them little notice.

"Join me," he said, gesturing to one of the empty tables. "You can tell me all about it. I'm a licensed thera- pist."

"You're a vicar."

"Near as dammit."

Kevin laughed and seated his bulk, pulling a hand- kerchief from his pocket and dabbing at his perspiring forehead. "The wife is not a happy bunny, that's all," he said.

"They often aren't."

"Yours, too?"

"Dead, I'm afraid."

"Sorry to hear that, mate … Vicar." He regarded Tom with sympathy, as if searching for some cue to continue in this vein, but the server arrived at that moment to take their order—cream tea for Tom, a single cuppa for Kevin. He gripped his bulging tummy with both hands. "This is what happens when you drive a coach all day."

"How long have you been doing it?"

"Near thirty years. I've seen more of the U.K. and Europe than most people will see in a lifetime."

"You've got one on me. Before I entered the priest-hood, I was a magician, and did a fair share of busking around the Continent, but—"

"But you weren't married then."

"No."

"This is why Val—that's the wife—isn't too chuffed. I've had a call to be a replacement driver on a ten-day tour of the Loire Valley. I used to do these a lot more in me younger days, but you know, I'm getting older, and Val doesn't like me away. Thinks I'll get up to mischief, or something."

"And would you?"

Kevin grinned. "Chance would be a fine thing. No, seriously, Vicar, I learned me lesson on that score, years back. Val's me second wife, if you catch me drift. And look at this?" He patted his stomach. "Who'd have me now? But, still, wives, you know…"

"Nice to have someone looking out for you."

"Yeah, that's true. Sorry," he said again, as if apologising for having a wife where Tom had none.

The refreshments arrived and they watched in silence as the tea things were placed on the table.

"You haven't always worked for Cooper's Coaches,

I'm guessing," Tom said as he sawed his scone in half. "You're from where—near Manchester?"

Kevin nodded. "Bolton. Got me first driving job there. Then we were outside London, near Luton, for a bit. Then came down here, what? Twenty years since, I guess. The wife wanted a quieter life. And housing were cheaper here—at least then."

"Did you happen to know Charley Rouse?" Tom spread clotted cream on his scone.

"Who just died? Yeah, a bit. You know, us drivers are mostly ships what pass in the night, so to speak, 'cept for the Christmas do the company puts on. Why do you ask?"

"I was at the reenactment where he died."

"Oh. Too bad, that. He were mad for that stuff, Charley. Daft bugger, really. I'll tell you what's sticks out in me mind about Charley Rouse. It's legend. The way he quit. He were taking a coach full of pensioners from Paignton to Gatwick. Supposed to be on a flight to ... I don't know where. Marbella? He'd have done the route a hundred times, down the A303, the M3, the M25, follow the signs, boom, you're there. Easy peasy.

"Bugger gets lost. Supposedly. Wandering about, up hill and down dale through Hampshire. Finally pulls in somewhere. Stockbridge, I think. The passengers are raving by this time. What does he do? He legs it. Leaves them high and dry. Opens the door, steps down, and pisses off into thin air. Doesn't even phone the company so they can find a replacement driver in the area. Are you going to eat that?"

Tom silently handed him the other half of the scone.

"Could I have your knife?"

"I expect the passengers didn't make their flights." Tom watched as Kevin slathered clotted cream and

58

strawberry preserve on the pastry and shoved it in his mouth.

"Not a one," Kevin gurgled, his mouth crammed.

"I'm assuming some sort of distress, a nervous breakdown, perhaps," Tom mused, lifting his cup to his lips.

Kevin shrugged. "Daft bugger, as I said, but he were a good driver. Least, far's I know. Some can't handle the job over long run. Takes all kinds. You're responsible for your passengers, but you've got no authority over them. Not sure which is worse. Lads after a football match, hen parties, or kids. Maybe kids. Don't get me wrong. I love mine to bits. You got kids?"

"One."

"But get a pack of 'em on a bus for an hour and you'll go mental." He stuffed the remainder of the scone in his mouth. "Charley were lucky on that score. He didn't have to put up with that."

"What? Driving children around?"

"Were in his contract."

"I had no idea such arrangements could be negotiated."

"They can." Kevin shrugged again. "Depending on circumstances. Creates a bit of resentment, though, 'special treatment' and all."

"I can imagine."

"In Charley's case, though …" Kevin paused, his mouth seeming to twist in indecision. He looked around the yard, at the others contentedly eating their teas. "In Charley's case, though," he repeated, lowering his voice, "I think there were another reason."

"For his contractual arrangements, you mean."

"Yeah. Look, I'll say this to you because you're a vicar and all, but …" He tapped the side of his nose and leaned across the table. "Between you, me and the lamp post, I think Charley were a bit of a kiddie fiddler."

"Don't often see you in here this time of day." Eric Swan eyed Tom over the glass he was polishing. "Madrun not got supper on the table?"

"I fancied a swift half."

"For Dutch courage?"

"What makes you say that?"

"Your face. Weight of the world. As if you're dreading going home because Madrun is going to give you a bollocking."

"Hardly that, Eric."

"Usual?"

Tom nodded. "Although …"

Eric raised a ginger eyebrow as he pulled the pump.

"…although Mrs. Prowse has been behaving a bit strangely the last few days."

"What? More than usual?" He placed the pint of Vicar's Ruin on a bar mat.

"Moot point, I suppose." Tom smiled and lifted his glass. He glanced at the pub quiz notice behind Eric's head. "I've spent the day leading a coach tour to Tintagel and Bodmin."

"Nice work if you can get it."

"Sorry." Tom knew how difficult it was for Eric to get a day off, what with running the Church House Inn seven days a week and four children underfoot.

"Or perhaps not so nice. You do look a bit off-colour, Tom."

"Well," Tom took a sip, savoured the bitter taste. "I had a disturbing conversation earlier in the day."

"Not related to the late Charley Rouse, by chance?"

Tom glanced up sharply. "How did you know?"

"A fair guess. But Roger did happen to mention the other day you were in the wrong place at the wrong time Saturday, at the annual Brawl of Thornford."

"Did he now."

Tom's mind returned to his conversation with Kevin, the coach driver. The man's imputation that Charley Rouse had a sexual interest in children had rendered him speechless for a moment though his mind roiled.

"Was nothing done about it?" he'd asked Kevin when he'd caught a breath.

"Don't know details." The man shrugged. "Charley were a good driver, as I said. Hard to find, them. And maybe it were hard to prove, whatever it were—I think a lass accused him of … well, you know. P'rhaps it were only that one time."

"A girl."

"Yeah, think so. Horrible, innit? Glad me kids are boys, though that don't mean—"

"Was this incident widely known? I mean, among your fellow drivers?"

"Not so's I know. No one said. And I didn't want to say. None of me business, really. But Charley sort of kept himself to himself after.

"Look, I only know what I know because I happened to be passing front office after a late run when boss were laying into Charley like he were a punching bag. The door were open a crack." Kevin looked like he regretted saying anything at all. "Maybe I got it wrong. But after that he stopped driving kids."

And then disappeared, Tom thought. "How much time passed between that incident and his abandoning the coach on the way to Gatwick?"

"Maybe a year? Little more, p'rhaps," Kevin considered. "Funny him pitching up here again after all this time. I never told the wife back then. She's the sort who gets in a right flap over anything. And I didn't need aggro at work. And it *were* hearsay, weren't it?"

Tom had agreed that it was, but he felt suddenly as if someone had yanked open a curtain and let sunshine pour into a darkened dusty room. He thought about Miranda, and about Eric's two daughters, Lucy and Emily. Jago had daughters, too, Tamara and Kerra, though they were young women now.

"And what was your disturbing conversation about, Tom?" Eric asked, breaking into his thoughts.

"Oh … let's see: the worrying challenges of raising children in today's world," he replied, thinking that sounded more like a chat show topic.

Eric drummed his fingers along the bar.

"What is it?" Tom looked up from his drink.

"Have you got a few more minutes?"

"Well …" he glanced at his glass.

"Come through to the back." Eric stepped away and called into the public bar where his wife was serving, "Belinda, I'm taking a short break, 'k?"

"Fine, luv. I'll cover," a voice floated back.

"I feel like I've been banished to the headmaster's study," he said to Eric when he'd taken a chair in the back room used for private functions. "I was caned once, you know. In the last days it was kosher."

"Once?" Eric snorted, with a rub at his backside. "I've still got bleedin' scars." He seated his bulk across from Tom. "Listen, there's something you should probably know …"

"Is this about Charley Rouse?" Tom prompted.

"Yes."

Tom studied Eric as he shifted uncomfortably in his seat. "If this is something unpleasant, then I think I know what it is. An informed source … okay, coach driver mate of Charley's told me something serious this afternoon." He paused to gather his wits. "Charley is … was, rather, suspected of being—" the word stuck on his lips "—a pedophile."

Eric locked eyes with him. "I would say 'suspected' is feeble."

"Please don't tell me your—"

"We only had Daniel and Lucy when moved down here to take on this pub. This is what? Nine years ago? But nine years ago Jago's girls were eleven or twelve or so, which seemed to be that sick bastard's preferred taste."

"Oh, God."

"It all came out here, in this very room, in fact. At a surprise birthday tea for Jago. It was Charley who got the surprise, though. Something twigged Jago to what Charley was up to. Your Madrun was there. Sharon, Charley's wife … you know her?"

"To see her."

"Maureen—"

"The girls?"

"Jago must have figured a way to get Kerra and Tamara out of the room when he blew up. He's got short fuse, you know that. I would have missed it, but ice cream for Jago's cake had gone forgotten, so I'd phoned Roger, and he trotted over with some from his shop, and we, the two of us, Roger and me, entered here, this room, together…" Eric paused, as if in memory. "I mean, you could hear shouting down the passage, but not words…"

63

Tom frowned. "Yes …?"

"Jago had Charley in a throat hold and was squeezing the life out of him, called him a 'pedo', threatened to kill him if he ever saw the likes of him again. He had been molesting Kerra. Roger and I were able to pull Jago off him. Charley buggered off sharpish." Eric's mouth twisted. "Never saw him again."

"And now he's dead," Tom reflected.

"We thought he might have died long since."

"What? You mean … that Jago carried out his threat?"

"A day or two later Charley walked off the job, that's what his boss told Sharon. Abandoned his passengers on the way to Gatwick or Heathrow …" Eric paused as Tom nodded. "You know this, too, then."

"But that happened a hundred miles from here. Jago—"

"Tom, Sharon never had any calls after, no emails, no texts. No money taken from their account at a cashpoint. No activity on credit cards."

"She didn't report him missing?"

"No."

"To spare Jago's girls—or any others—having to testify and relive the horror?"

Eric nodded. "That, yes. And Sharon runs a childminding service, remember. Having a pedo for a husband? No one wanted him around, Tom. Best he was gone, however he was gone."

"So," Tom ran his finger absently around the top of his glass, "you've thought—all of you—all these years that Jago might have gone after Charley, might have …" He left the rest unsaid.

"We didn't know. We put it out of your minds. Those of us in this room that day didn't make a secret pact or

64

anything like that, but none of us has ever breathed it to another soul."

"Until now."

"Until now.

"But this time Charley Rouse truly is dead."

6

Thursday

The sign's letters were faded and Buttles Caravan Park's reception area wasn't much more than a shed beside a farm gate, but the fleshy woman minding it was as vigilant as a watch dog. Tom's clerical collar persuaded her he wasn't the repo man or the VAT inspector and grudgingly gave him directions to Dania Bloczynski's caravan—not that he couldn't have found it on his own: it was the only one sat next to a car decorated with a Polish flag logo—and, oddly, a Scottish one.

"Tell her she needs to make up her mind sharpish," the manageress called after him. "I could hire out that spot twice over!"

He didn't doubt it. The park was unkempt, but hardly empty. The price of housing, he knew, obliged more and more people into these unprepossessing homes, and he was grateful—nay, conscience-stricken—for the grand home he'd found himself living in.

A thin woman with hair the colour of straw was leaning against a peeling blue caravan, smoking a cigarette and staring into the middle distance. She turned her head as

Tom approached and hastily stubbed her cigarette under her sandal. She was wearing white shorts and a red T-shirt with BLACK ISLAND BREWING clearly readable on it. Her face was pinched and pale, untouched by the sun they'd had this summer in the West Country. Her eyes darted to him nervously until they, like the manageress's earlier, came to rest on his dog collar. Relief, with a little perplexity, flooded her face.

Tom introduced himself, offered traditional words of condolence. "I wondered," he finished, "how I might be of service."

"Oh," she responded doubtfully. "I … there is so much to do. I … with Charley gone. And the lady in the office …"

"I know. She is rather abrupt, isn't she?" He glanced at the caravan and its possibility of privacy. He said gently, "Might it be a good idea to go inside and have a cup of tea?"

"Of course. Please, yes, come in."

The interior of the caravan was tidy, but there seemed to be clothes everywhere. Tom watched as Dania pushed aside a pile of folded trousers to furnish him a seat and stepped to the compact kitchen to fill a kettle over the tiny sink.

"Are you packing or unpacking?" he asked.

"I don't know. I don't know what I'm doing. I started to go through Charley's clothes. He will need something for the … for the …"

"Funeral," Tom supplied.

"But the police …"

"I understand," Tom said. The police had not yet released the body, which was suggestive of ongoing investigation.

"I don't know what my Charley would want. I don't

68

know where his people are, if there are any. His parents are dead, he said. No brothers, no sisters. He is an orphan it seems. But I think his people are from around here. They must be. He has the West Country accent." She plugged in the kettle. "No, I will take him back to Inverness … or not. I don't know. The police are no help."

"You're from Inverness then," Tom slipped in.

"Yes. I am Polish, though. You can tell? I moved to Scotland with my parents when Poland joined the EU. My father was a teacher in Lublin but there was more money working in a salmon factory in the Highlands, did you know that? He has gone back, though. With my mother. He did not care anymore for the stink of fish."

"Things are better in Poland now."

Dania shrugged. "I don't know."

"You're not—"

"My child is a Scottish girl. I am not going back to Poland." A hard expression came over her thin face. "My parents were not happy …"

"About?" Tom prompted.

"I did not marry Lily's father. Lily is my daughter. My parents are very—how do you say?—conservative, Catholic. You see?"

"But a grandchild …"

Dania made a dismissive gesture, pulled a packet of Jaffa cakes from a shelf over the sink. "Charley was so kind. He did not care about such things. Like modern people. He loves Lily like she were his own. He is … was—" the words seemed to catch in her throat—"her true father."

Tom felt a stone drop in his stomach as he watched Dania gravely setting out the biscuits on a plate. Did she know nothing of his past? Sense anything about his proclivities? *Could he have reformed? Was it possible?*

69

Everything he knew—and read from the church's own study and commissions—indicated that men such as Charley struggled in their own hells and with great difficulty quelling their impulses.

He took a cleansing breath. "Where did you meet Charley?"

"In Inverness. He taught me how to drive. He was a driving instructor, you see. That's how we met." The kettle shrieked. She switched it off and poured the steaming water into a teapot. "I thought I should learn. My parents left me their car when they returned to Poland. Right-hand drive, you see? Doesn't work so good in Europe."

"Where is your daughter, by the way?"

"She is with a nice lady who lives here, in the park. They've gone to the beach for a few hours." She swirled the pot and placed it on the table. "Gives me some time to be by myself and think."

"Won't you return to Inverness then?"

"I don't know. Perhaps. But, you see, we decided to leave Inverness. Well, Charley's idea, but I thought, yes, why not? Go somewhere where there is more sun. Scotland, you know. Clouds, always clouds. Milk?"

"Please, yes."

She bent down to the tiny refrigerator. He glimpsed the hollows along the spine at the back of her neck and thought how vulnerable she seemed. He said as she rose:

"Then your intent, I gather, was to settle somewhere else."

"Yes, we bought this caravan ..." She shot the interior a doubtful glance as she handed Tom the milk jug "...to spend the summer break travelling, live like gypsies, you know? Before, Charley would go to these reenactments— he is crazy for these things—on his own, but we decided to go together, with Lily. We would go to them … well, *he* would go to them—"

"You didn't attend?"

"Lily and I went once, to one near York. It was very silly. I didn't say that to Charley."

"You weren't at the one here last Saturday, then?" Tom poured milk into the bottom of the mug set before him.

Dania's face crumpled. "If only I had. Things might have been different, yes? I was going to go to this one, Charley wanted me to, it was the last of the season, he said, and my nice neighbour—she is a lesbian, I think, but that's okay—was going to take Lily to the beach—Lily loves the beach—but she had to change her plans, so I took Lily to Breakwater Beach and look what happened!"

"I'm sorry."

"I'm sorry, too," Dania said gravely, lifting the pot and pouring tea into Tom's mug. "Now do I stay here? I have to enroll Lily in a school—school starts next week, oh god— and find some work."

"You cleaned house for Venice Dainty."

"She is a nice lady. Her sister not so much."

"Sister-in-law."

Dania grunted, sat down across from Tom, reached for a mug of her own and began pouring. "I cleaned houses in Inverness for a while. It doesn't pay so good."

"Are you trained for anything?"

"Bar maid? Shop assistant? I was not good in school. My parents were not happy with this. Lily must not become like me."

Tom could think of three primary schools in the vicinity, but all were C of E and all, including the one in Thornford, terribly oversubscribed, with fierce parents vigilant over queue-jumpers. Should he, he wondered, put

71

in a word with the headmistress at Thornford Primary?

"Let me see if there's anything I can do … about schooling," he said, adding hastily as her face brightened, "I can't promise anything. And you might find work at—" He stopped himself. The suggestion he was about to make was fraught; Charley's estranged wife managed the child-minding service. But it was too late.

"At where?" Dania regarded him eagerly, looking up from her steaming mug.

"At the farm shop at Thorn Barton. I know they're often looking for staff."

"You are a good man, Father Christmas." Sudden laughter lit up her face. "*Father Christmas*, ha! You are Father Christmas to me, bringing me these presents."

"Well, I like to be of some use," Tom stifled a blush, ears alert suddenly to the crunch of wheels on crushed stone.

Dania looked past Tom's shoulder to the window. He noted her smile wither.

"Lily is back. She will see you. You are a priest."

"Yes …?"

"She will wonder."

"You mean," Tom set his tea down. "You haven't told her."

"No. I …"

"How old is she?"

"Twelve in a few months."

"I'm sure she must sense something," Tom said gently, reflecting how quickly Miranda, at seven, had intuited that her mother was not returning. "Was she not here when the police visited?"

"No, she was at the beach. I told her Charley had some business in Plymouth. Though she is starting to wonder ..."

"Would you like me to leave?"

Dania's hand went to a cigarette pack at the side of the table. She fingered it nervously. "No. It is time."

Footfalls tapped on the metal steps outside. Tom turned his head and formed his lips into a welcoming smile. But the child who stepped into the light of the interior was so arrestingly beautiful he almost gaped. Her face was as pale as her mother's and she shared some of Dania's particulars—deep-set eyes and high cheekbones—but in a fresh and flawless proportion that surely owed something to the absent father. Green eyes, cupid's-bow lips, and ginger-coloured hair fell in ringlets to a T-shirt that hinted—Tom had to glance away—at budding womanhood, and in that moment he realised, sickeningly, the allure this uncommon child could have had to the likes of Charley Rouse, and how, by someone's intervention, she may well have been spared his prurient attentions.

"Hello," he greeted her warmly, but the girl, her expression solemn, searched out her mother's eyes, ignoring his greeting, moving quickly to Dania's outstretched arms.

"We have a visitor," Dania said, turning her to face Tom.

But a rustle of movement by the door arrested Tom's attention. A voice with gravel in it called out, "We stopped at the Co-op. I brought some cherries back for you."

Something about voice, its timbre, tugged at Tom's memory, and when the voice's owner, a sturdy young woman dressed in short khakis and a slouch hat, stepped into the cabin, his sense of displacement intensified. He had seen her, met her before, somewhere, but the occasion remained tantalisingly out of reach. Her eyes roved to him. He saw from her surprise that she was not expecting anyone else to be in the cabin, but in that surprise he thought he saw a flash of recognition.

But the sensation vanished as quickly as it had arrived.

"Thank you," Dania said to the woman. "And thank you for taking Lily to the beach again. This is Tom Christmas. Will you have a cup of—?"

"Another time, thanks," she responded, dropping a carrier bag on the floor. "Must dash! Good to meet you," she addressed Tom as she turned back toward the steps.

"And you," Tom called after her. "Not that I caught her name," he added to Dania. "She seems a bit anxious."

"Her name's Elliott. She is so kind to us. She takes Lily on her motorbike, so exciting, and it is safe. Lily has her own helmet." Dania hugged the girl who seemed to fold into her arms. "Elliott works at Asda and gets the employee discount so she is very helpful."

"Which Asda?"

"Newton Abbott."

"Ah."

The young woman in the green gilet in the Asda parking floated into his mind. That explained her familiarity. But why did her voice resonate so?

Supper—Madrun's very good baked salmon and roasted sweet potatoes—was done and Miranda gone to play with Swan kids down at the millpond when Jago arrived by the side door carrying a typewriter.

"Sorry it took so long, Maddy," he said to his sister, plunking her red Olivetti on the kitchen table. Tom, at the counter pouring himself a cup of coffee, knew something was amiss when he turned to see Jago quick to retreat rather than sniff around for a bit of his sister's baking.

74

"Wait, Jago! I wonder if I might have a word," he said, noting a wary look pass between his housekeeper and her brother.

"Well … I've got Sharon with me." Tom could hear the reluctance in his tone. "We're on our way to the pub."

"The quiz doesn't start for nearly an hour. Why don't you both come in and have some of your sister's superb gooseberry tart? There's still some left from Saturday. Or a drink here first, perhaps."

"Can't say no to that," Jago said, but his smile fell short of his eyes. He stepped back through the boot room and calling to Sharon. Some muttered conversation ensued. Tom looked to Madrun but she'd turned her back to hook damp tea towels over the Aga handles.

Sharon trailed Jago into the kitchen. She was a rounded and motherly woman, her curves obscured by a loose cotton dress, her short hair strongly streaked with grey. Her expression was gentle, but it was shadowed by strain, as if forbearance were her Cross.

"I hope you don't mind my asking you to come in," he began, gesturing to seats at the table. "I thought we might have a better chance for a good conversation away from the pub noise and such. Mrs. Prowse, would you care to—"

"If it's all the same with you, Mr. Christmas, now my typewriter's back…"

"Yes, I see."

"Say 'hi' to Mum for me, Maddy," Jago teased.

"I always do, Jago," Madrun called over her shoulder.

"There's fresh coffee, and there's still tea in the pot," Tom offered. "Though it's probably a bit stewed by now."

Jago heaved a sigh, shot Tom a glum glance. "I think that a drink's in order. Brandy, if you've got it, Tom. Sharon?"

Sharon nodded. Tom went to the drinks cabinet in the dining room and fetched the brandy and three snifters. When he returned the two had seated themselves.

"You're not going to let this alone, are you?" Jago hunched over the table, watching Tom pour the amber liquid.

"A man is dead, Jago."

"And bloody good job, too!"

Tom watched Sharon slide a calming hand to Jago's arm and wondered at the depth of her feelings. "I understand your anger," he said. "I understand it *now*. I do. And," he added holding up a restraining hand as Jago eyed him unhappily, "it doesn't matter how I know or who may have told me."

"They should keep their bloody mouths shut."

"They have, they did, but circumstances have changed."

"It was a freak accident, papers said. Nothing to do with me."

"Jago, I think the police will come to another conclusion before very long, if they haven't already."

"Well, then, it wasn't me who marked his card." Jago drowned his brandy in a single gulp. "Look, Vicar, you know—*now*—and I know and Roger knows and Eric knows and half the bloody village—"

"Half the village doesn't, surprisingly. This is one secret the few have managed to keep."

"—that I told Charley I'd kill him if he didn't get shot of here and never show his bloody face again. Well, I was glad he came back. It proved to some folk I hadn't done him in all those years ago. I said those words in the pub in the moment, like you do, but I've had funny looks since from certain folk ever after. It was the beginning of the end with Maureen. Even my own sister sometimes, for God's sake …

"And, *and!*" Jago stabbed the air. "I even have an alibi for the day Charley abandoned that coach on the way to the airport—you know about that—?"

Tom nodded.

"—not that anyone bothered to ask. I had a job at Noze Lydiard Castle. I have the records and I can find the prat who ran off the drive into a tree if I have to."

"I'm sure that's true." Tom glanced again at Sharon who, throughout this exchange, kept her hand firmly on Jago's arm, though her eyes remained fixed on the table-cloth, her brandy untouched. "But I'm not sure it matters now—now that Charley isn't missing, but dead. Police are going to start looking more closely at family and friends of the deceased. They'll find out you were at the reenactment from someone—"

"You?"

"Only if I'm asked, Jago." Tom lifted his snifter and sipped. "But I won't be the only person to clock you there, then. What really took you to the Battle of Thornford?"

"I told you. A service call."

Tom glanced at Sharon, who lifted her eyes to Tom's. She nudged Jago's arm.

"Best tell him, Jago," she sighed.

"Jesus," Jago muttered. "Okay, I drove Sharon there. That's why I was there." He reached for the brandy bottle and poured an inch. "Look, Tom, it was the only place we knew we could find him. The bugger wouldn't tell Sharon where he was stopping."

Tom thought he knew why. Sharon would have seen his living arrangements. Met Dania. Glimpsed the angelic child. "I expect," he said gently to Sharon, "minds more

77

suspicious than mine will wonder why you wanted to find Charley."

"It's simple, Father—"

"Tom, please."

"It's simple, Tom. I had a Form E and other papers to give him. That's all, really," she added, as if Tom's expression registered doubt. "I'd begun divorce proceedings years back, but Charley had vanished. As there had been no contact for more than seven years, I was about ready to have him declared legally dead. But as I'd learned he was alive, I knew if there were a reenactment in the picture he'd be there."

"And did you find him?"

"No. We arrived late, near the end of the battle. I looked, but then there was a rumour going about that someone had died, in the woods and I knew, just knew, that it was Charley."

"A description from someone in the crowd," Jago added glumly, "of a very tall bloke. Charley was very tall. Charley Longshanks, he was called sometimes."

"We left," Sharon said murmured, cupping the snifter as if warming her hands, but not drinking.

"We left, Tom," Jago added for emphasis, locking eyes with Tom. "Slipped away."

Tom's mind returned to the terrible event, Barbara emerging from the edge of the Wood, her surplice clutched to her chest, a look of anguish on her face. Morchard Wood was one of the last bits of ancient woodland in the county, dense and tangled. Who else might have been in that wood those vital moments? He regarded Jago and Sharon, hoping that they were not marvelous dissemblers concocting a tale. Where had Sharon been the whole time? He had not seen her standing with Jago at the battle itself.

"The mystery," he said, "is why Charley reappeared at all. Forms, papers, the legal minutia you mentioned, Sharon, could be done at a distance." He paused. "He met with you up at Thorn Barton recently. That's when you knew he'd returned."

"How did you know?"

"Jeanette told me when I visited her in hospital the other day."

"I suppose she said we were quarrelling."

"Well, raised voices."

"Imagine my shock, Tom. He'd vanished from my life, and suddenly he's standing right in front of me. I'd never had the chance to give him a piece of my mind." Her arm left Jago's. She paused as if considering her next words. "He wanted to be forgiven."

"For walking out on you? For—?"

"For that ... and for ..." Sharon glanced at Jago whose jaw clamped tight. "You see, I had had no idea about Charley's ... bent until that fight years ago at the pub when Jago—"

"Gave him the thrashing he deserved." Jago crossed his arms with sudden force.

"Charley acknowledged," she continued, "that he ... liked children—girls when they're ... oh, God—"

"Take your time."

"—liked them when they're preadolescent. He said he had had therapy, that he was part of a support group, like AA, that he didn't act on his desires. He said he was now what he called a 'virtuous pedophile.'"

"Absolute bloody bollocks!" Jago exploded.

Tom looked down at his hands sensing Sharon searching his face. He had spent the afternoon wrestling with his Sunday sermon, the theme of which, taken from

Matthew 18.21-35, was the limits of forgiveness. *Then Peter came to Jesus and asked, "Lord, how many times shall I forgive my brother or sister who sins against me? Up to seven times?" Jesus answered, "I tell you, not seven times, but seventy-seven times.*

Forgive as many times as is necessary, Jesus seems to be saying, though he might have been giving Peter a little dig for seeking rules to bind life, Tom thought as he typed first thoughts. However, nowhere in Scripture does forgiveness mean treating someone as if he had never sinned. Forgiveness doesn't cancel the real need for justice. It doesn't indulge injury or insult. Repentance comes first.

Charley Rouse's situation wasn't the first he'd had to contend with. In Bristol, there'd been a man in his congregation accusing of molesting boys. Was reform possible? And yet Charley had not vouchsafed to his estranged wife that he was living with a woman who had a child herself on the cusp of adolescence. And he had not, if he read Dania at all correctly, vouchsafed his fraught past to *her*.

"And did you forgive him?" Tom asked Sharon.

"No."

"Too bloody right you didn't," Jago muttered.

"I couldn't, Tom. I'm a licensed childminder, for one thing, Tom. How could I? What Charley did ... does is utterly repellent to me. I thought he was simply being nice to Kerra—she's his niece after all, but then Jago told me how ..." She took a deep breath. "Anyway, I should have been more alert. Part of our training to watch out for signs of abuse. But with Charley I was oblivious. We couldn't have children of our own, you see, so I thought he was just compensating ..." she trailed off, her voice rimed with despair. "It's all so sick and sad."

"Did you believe him, then? Believe him when he said

he'd committed no more offences?"

"I don't know, I don't." Her voice was strained. She peered into the middle distance as if, perhaps, trying to conjure up their encounter at Thorn Barton. "Do you? Is it possible?"

"I don't know either," Tom shook his head.

"You're a priest," Jago interjected.

"That doesn't mean I have all the answers at hand, Jago. I struggle with this, too. 'Have no fellowship with the unfruitful works of darkness'—Ephesians—'but rather reprove them.' But a proclivity that can lead to such very grave sin makes me wonder why God would create someone to be sexually attracted to children."

"Born this way, you mean," he snapped.

"I don't know, Jago. There are alcoholics who never touch alcohol. But they remain alcoholics. Perhaps there are pedophiles who never touch children—"

"Look, I'm not having some bloody churchy palaver. A pedophile who touches a child is a child molester, a monster. Charley *molested* Kerra. Your Miranda is what? eleven? Think about it. What would you do?"

"I wouldn't kill the offender, Jago."

"I didn't bloody kill Charley Rouse!"

A uncomfortable silence descended over the kitchen. Tom's ears went to the faint tap tap tap of Madrun's typewriter in her aerie above. Was she writing her mother about *this*? (Writing loved ones reminded him that he owed an email to his Honorary Father in Gravesend.)

"Sorry," said Jago after a moment. "I've tried to tell Sharon that avoiding prosecution—'cause it wasn't too late, you know—is the reason he was on this … this pedo apology tour—"

"Do you mean," Tom interrupted, startled, "that he

was going around visiting the people he'd hurt, or was planning to go around?"

"I don't know," Sharon shrugged. "Honestly, I don't. I don't know if he saw anyone else. That's Jago's interpretation."

"And he wouldn't bloody have gotten anywhere near my Kerra, that's for certain!"

"And I'm not sure she would want this stirred up, Jago," Sharon reflected.

"How is Kerra?" Tom asked. Unprompted came the thought that it was Kerra, not Roger, who had gasped at the Sunday service when he'd said Charley's name. She was the youngest member of the choir, a quiet girl, not as exuberant as her older sister Tamara. *Was there lasting damage?*

"She's ... fine," Jago answered. "I sussed what that bastard was up to before it got too far."

"It was all very odd, in a way," Sharon said. "I wonder now if Charley hadn't some sort of premonition. For instance, he told me pointedly I was the beneficiary of reenactment insurance he's been paying into all these years. I had no idea he'd ever had such insurance. But perhaps it was part of the ..."

"Contrition?" Tom supplied, studying her face. That she'd been so quick to investigate the claim after her husband's death gave him pause. Did she and Jago know that the insurance only paid out if death were accidental? Did some scheme depend on Charley's death appearing to be so? Regarded in a cold light, Jago and Sharon had opportunity and more than a single motive. And the means was to hand at the reenactment.

His mind went back to Jago's earlier expression. "If there were this ... tour, as you called it," he began, almost dreading the revelation, "then who else ...? How many—"

"Not like he had a bloody harem, Tom," Jago interrupted, his face darkening. "Least as far as I know." He turned to Sharon. "There was that girl that used to live over the road from yours in Hamlyn."

"Elise Coaker," Sharon supplied.

"Barbara's younger sister," said Tom, remembering—but now in a different light—his sister-in-law's story about Charley fetching her from school.

"You know her?" Sharon asked.

"She's newly priest at All Saint's."

"I'd heard she'd gone into the Church, but—"

"You'll see her again shortly. She's part of the Hamlyn Quizzards team. You didn't see her name on the roster?"

"No. It's Jago who signed us up." Sharon blanched. "Oh, God. I wonder if Barbara knows ..."

"She was at the reenactment. She and I were both called on for our priestly duties. Did you not see her?"

"No. We arrived late, as Jago said." Sharon at last took a sip of brandy. "Years ago, in the aftermath, after Charley vanished, I worried about Elise, but she was gone by then. Barbara had gone off to university, and Elise gone to ... some reluctant cousin around Kingswear, I think, though she still went to Hamlyn Grammar." She wiped at the brandy on her lip. "You see, Elise lived with us, with Charley and me, for a short time earlier. Their mother was long gone and their father, never up to the job anyway, died when Elise was around twelve. Rather than being taken into care, we took her in while other arrangements with the cousin were being made."

"Do you know where the sister is today?" Jago turned to Sharon.

"I don't know where she lives. But I know where she

83

works, or at least where she worked a month ago, when I ran into her shopping. God, thinking about what Charley might have done, I could hardly look at her, and it's not because she was starting … what do you call it? Transitioning?"

"Transitioning?" Jago jerked his head. "From what—?"

"From a female to a male."

"Bloody hell. If my girls ever—"

"Where does she work?" Tom straightened in his chair, newly alert.

"At the Asda, in Newton Abbot."

Horses sweat, men perspire, and women glow, Tom thought unaccountably, distracting himself as he hurried past the loose, chatty groups on the benches outside the Church House Inn, their smiling faces shiny in the heated air. The deepening evening had an enchanted end-of-summer quality, a golden pause before autumn's inevitable chilly grip, and Tom would have savoured it in other circumstances, would have delighted in the pub quiz, too, as he was not half bad at it, but this evening his heart was freighted with sadness, and not a little apprehension.

The saloon bar, he saw immediately as he stepped over the threshold, was heaving, and this was one gladdening note at least, as it meant this fundraising effort at least would not be for naught. Mark Tucker, squashed into the corner nearest the fireplace where he and the rest of the Thornford Irregulars were poring over the quiz sheet, called to him cheerily, "You're late!" Second time in a week.

Tom apologised as the others shuffled their chairs to give him room to sit and cast his eyes over the room. On the other side, under the three-hundred-year-old mummified cat in a framed box, Barbara Coaker sat with several men and women, her team, the Hamlyn Quizzards presumably. Her eyes, too, were ranging over the interior with its moulded beams and horses brasses, but when they met with Tom's she swiftly returned her head to her quiz sheet, without acknowledging his presence. But in that fleeting connection, Tom was certain he witnessed more than simply a trace of pre-competition jitters. He wanted to go to her, lead her away from the thrum and racket, to somewhere quiet and safe—at least for a while—but Eric had slapped a pint of Vicar's Ruin in front of him and was already booming greetings to all, microphone in hand, reminding them of the rules of the game: eight rounds, double your points on any round other than the music round by showing your joker, and *all phones out of sight!*

"Without further ado, let's head straight on with round one—'FAITH AND BEGORRAH'." Eric attempted an Irish brogue. "Any jokers? No?"

"Odds are this hasn't anything to do with the Irish," Mark whispered in Tom's ear, passing him a biro to write down the answers.

"All right then," Eric continued. "All questions in this round relate to minced oaths." He looked up from his iPad. "That's 'euphemisms' to you lot. Milder versions of words you were never to say in front of your sainted grannies—or at least until Johnny Rotten uttered a certain word on afternoon telly some years back."

"And what word would that be, Eric?" someone shouted from the crowd.

"This is a respectable boozer, mate. Now, on with the game. An easy one to start you off. Question one: A cliché of how nineteenth-century Irish spoke, 'begorrah' is a euphemism for what expression?"

The answer hissed around Tom's table. "An easy one

indeed," he said, scribbling the answer in the allotted space: *By God*

"Question two: what light but binding supper dish might you best serve to the Son of God?"

Potential answers hissed around other tables, but Tom glanced up at a sea of frowns around his, adding his own. Then he remembered the risotto Madrun had served the week before. He wrote: *Cheese and Rice*

"Are you sure?" Mark whispered.

"Sound it out," Tom replied.

"Ah."

The same sorts of questions filled out the rest of the round: the short form of "God's wounds" and "God's looks" and such like.

"Bless," said Roger, fanning his heat-flushed face with his hand, "or should I say 'Faith'? If the priest from Hamlyn weren't present, I'd say Eric's picked these questions to favour *us*."

Tom glanced over at the Hamlyn Quizzards. Barbara evinced none of her bravado when the two villages last squared off, Saturday, at the Battle of Thornford. Despite the warmth and the informality of the evening event, she was buttoned tightly into the same black cassock she'd worn at the reenactment.

This gave Tom pause.

He'd had an extraordinary moment earlier, in the vicarage kitchen, with Jago and Sharon. *The Asda in Newton Abbot*, Sharon said, and in that minute Madrun's typewriter stopped dead, Bumble, his Jack Russell, padded into the room, and outside, in the community orchard next door, a child cried out. All in a rush the resolution to Rouse's death came to him.

Or so he thought.

Now he doubted the certainty of that moment. Was not life full of doubt?

He looked again at Barbara and thought back to the battle, as he had many times over the last days, his mind's eye on her emerging from edge of Morchard Wood. In memory, she burst forth from the undergrowth in a magpie flurry of black cassock and white surplice, as that had been her garb at the service. But now he more clearly saw her as crow, not magpie—in black worsted, her surplice clutched like a bundle of laundry tight to her chest. He presumed she'd removed it to ease the act of relieving herself outdoors, but had she removed it for another reason? He saw himself as he had Sunday morning, in front of the mirror, staunching the blood where he'd nicked himself shaving with one of the clean white towels landed in his bathroom. He had rolled it up and dropped it on a chair, with every good intention to remove the stain before it set—after the Sunday service and before Madrun did the next laundry. He never did.

Round Four was called. Roger read out loud: WHO'S A NAUGHTY BOY, THEN?

"A canine category?" Mark muttered as Eric returned the microphone to his mouth.

"Another easy one to start off with," the landlord announced, reading from his tablet. "'This Conservative politician's career ended in 1963 after it was revealed he had had a sexual relationship with nineteen-year-old model who was also bedding a Soviet spy.'"

Mark and the others looked blank. Tom thought he knew, but Roger, older than everyone, whispered confirmation in his ear. He dutifully wrote: *John Profumo.*

The rest of the round proceeded apace. Answers:

Jeremy Thorpe, Jeffrey Archer, John Major, the Prince of Wales. Dismayingly, naughty boys in public life abounded, and Tom rather wished this topic hadn't found its way into the quiz, as it Venn-diagrammed its way into his current apprehension.

"Wherever," he asked Eric in the fourth-round break for folk to use the loo and fetch drinks, "did you find that last category?"

"My *Boy's Own Book of British Pub Quizzes,*" Eric grinned, as he put another pint glass under a spout and pulled the lever. "Okay, the internet. Why?"

Tom didn't reply. From the corner of his eye, he glimpsed DI Bliss and DS Blessing stepping through the door, their suited selves suggesting they weren't out for an evening's stroll. His eyes darted to Barbara's seat. It was empty.

"Did you happen to see where Barbara Coaker went, the priest from Hamlyn?" he asked Eric in a low voice.

"Try the ladies'," was the reply. Eric nodded toward the back of the pub. "Here," he continued, shifting his body to block Tom from view of the door. "Shall I fend them off, those two coppers?"

"Please, yes."

Tom slipped into the back where the inn's toilets were situated across a narrow passageway that joined the road outside the pub.

"Bog's free, mate," said a man exiting the gents', casting him a suspicious glance for loitering outside the ladies'. Tom had no retort. At last the usual gurgles and splashes ceased and Barbara stepped out. She glanced at him with dismay.

"Come with me," he whispered, leading her down the passage to the road.

"But—"

"Never mind the quiz."

Silently Tom led her down the road, through The Square and around, into the churchyard the back way, down the pea shingle path to the ancient yew tree. Its vast trunk had a stone surround. He invited her to sit.

"I expect we don't have long," he said, studying her face shadowed now by the canopy of the enormous old tree. "The police have arrived at the pub."

"I see." Barbara's mouth folded into a controlled line. "And would that be for me, I wonder?"

"I can't think who else, I'm sorry, Barbara," he said, though Jago and Sharon flitted across his mind. "At the very least, they're only here seeking further help with their enquiries."

"And possibly more?"

"That they're here, at this time of evening, does suggest they're farther along in their investigations."

"Have you arrived at a conclusion?"

"No, I haven't," Tom replied after a pause. "But I can understand what might drive a person to—"

"Take the life of someone? To get to the point, Tom. Otherwise this conversation is a little oblique."

Tom looked though the yew's gnarled, tangled branches toward the marshaled gravestones pale gold lozenges in the last of the day's sun and took a cleansing breath. "I can think of little in the world more heinous than the abuse of a child. Yes, I know about it. I know what Charley Rouse did to at least a couple of children." When she didn't respond, he asked: "Did you know he was going to be at the reenactment?"

"I suspected he might be."

"Your sister told you he was back in the county, yes?"

"You've met my sister, I understand."

89

Tom hesitated. "I met her earlier today, yes."

Barbara gave him a searching glance, as if intuiting the words were true, but the answer incomplete.

"Do you think," she asked, "that the police know about Rouse's transgressions? Crimes, I should say."

"I suspect no one has told them—yet. For several people in Charley's past his transgressions—crimes—would be a strong motive to ..." He trailed off, glancing at the moon, beginning its rise over the millpond. "But eventually they'll dig out motives. It's early days in their investigation. I expect they may now have some physical evidence, something from the usual arsenal—fingerprints, blood sample, DNA—that's turning someone into a person of interest." He paused. "You told them, I think, that you didn't know the victim. They may know by now that you once lived across the road from him in Hamlyn."

Her next words jolted him:

"They'll find my fingerprints on the pike staff."

"You're certain," he said.

"I picked it up from the ground and shoved it through the back of Rouse's neck when he wasn't looking."

"I see." Tom swallowed. Her calm was preternatural. "But wouldn't ..." he began, almost for something to say, "wouldn't the force push him forward, onto his face?"

"No. He made a forward step, but his foot snagged on something."

"The badger hole you mentioned at the St. John's Ambulance tent."

"Yes," she responded after a moment. "At any rate, he fell backwards and broke the shaft as he fell and ... you saw the rest."

"That's very detailed." *And as his daughter had suspected, Charley had not secured his pike in any badger hole; it had served his demise in another way.*

Barbara turned to him. "Why wouldn't it be?

Tom met her eyes. *Did she do it, or did she see it done?* He continued: "Then you removed your surplice because blood was on it."

"Yes."

"You're certain."

"Yes, Tom."

"I see." Tom looked away. "You were angry."

"If one is angry in accordance with right reason, one's anger is deserving of praise."

The words were actorly, rehearsed, but familiar. Tom searched his memory. "Aquinas."

Barbara was silent.

"May I ask this? Why then did you close Charley's eyes?"

"What?"

"Charley's eyes. They were closed. I may be wrong, but in my experience most people *very* ill, in a coma say, die with their eyes closed. Or if they die in their sleep. But if death is sudden their eyes remain open. Charley died suddenly, horribly. But his eyes were closed. You closed them. It was, I can only think, an act of ... mercy or forgiveness, possibly? Pity, perhaps? At any rate, not the action of a killer."

"It's simply what I would do at a deathbed. Force of habit. I'm a priest."

"You are a priest. That's why I don't believe you would do this, or could so this. I think, at the very least, you *found* Charley Rouse dead. Or you may have been witness to his death. But you did not kill him." *And did you deliberately place your fingerprints on the staff?*

"Nonsense. I've told you what happened. I came upon

91

Rouse … doing his business and the red mist came down. I picked up his weapon with barely a thought and that was the end of it. Don't tell me …" She spoke with crisp fury, her eyes flashing through her spectacles, "Don't tell me, Tom Christmas, that I didn't have right reason."

"Doesn't Aquinas say something along the lines that *evil* may be found in anger when anger is either more or less than right reason demands? That—"

Anger leading to murder has no justification, he was about to say, but he was suddenly alert to footfalls approaching on the shingle. Barbara evidently heard them, too. She stiffened, bowed her head. "I'm confessing to it, Tom," she whispered. "That's the end of it. I should have done so at the very beginning."

A light step, not two men, not even one, Tom thought, and then a single shadowed figure ducked under the yew's heavy limbs.

"Elise!" Barbara said, squinting in the dim light. "What—"

"'Elliott', *please*, Barb."

"Yes, of course, I'm sorry. How did you—?"

"The landlord said you might be here."

"But why—?"

"I've been calling and texting, but—"

"My phone!" Barbara reached into the inside depths of her cassock. "The quiz. We had to switch our phones off. I didn't feel the vibration. What's happened? I thought you were with the dogs at my cottage."

"I was, but two men came to the door, detectives from Totnes CID. Stupidly I said you were here, in Thornford, at the pub. I came as fast as I could to warn—"

"How did you get here?"

"My motorbike."

"So dangerous!"

"Are Bliss and Blessing inside?" Tom asked, studying the face he'd only glimpsed in the past. It was plain, like Barbara's—round, feminine, really; none would doubt her sex, few would heed the alto voice, nor, he thought, casting his eyes lower, the short khakis or the close-cropped hair.

"What?" Elliott seemed to notice Tom for the first time. The flicker of anxiety she'd exhibited that afternoon in Dania's caravan flamed in agitation.

"The detectives, DI Bliss and DS Blessing."

"I don't know, I don't think so. The landlord sent me out the back." She looked at Tom askance, then locked eyes on her sister. "What do they want, Barb?"

Barbara groaned.

Tom supplied the answer: "The truth."

A silence fell, broken only by the splash of a diving bird penetrating the millpond's surface. Farther off, over the churchyard's high stone wall, drifted faint notes of some pop tune, the musical question for the fifth round, the signal that quiz night was continuing without their presence. The two women seemed yoked in private agony: Tom could hear Barbara's heavy breaths, and then, her final gulp of air as she rose from her seat. "I'm going to turn myself in, Elliott."

"But you can't."

"It's only a matter of time." She folded her sister into her arms. "They'll have everything they need … and before long they'll have the motive."

Elliott's eyes flicked anxiously past Barbara's shoulder to Tom.

"He knows," Barbara said, releasing Elliott, holding her firmly by the elbow. "He knows what Rouse did to you. He knows why I did what I did."

"That's not the truth, Barbara," Tom interjected, his heart heavy.

"It *is* the truth. Elliott was not even *at* the reenactment, nowhere near, so how could—"

"But, Barbara," Tom shot up from the stone seat, vertigo suddenly gripping him, disorienting him momentarily. "She *was* at the reenactment." He snatched at a tree branch for balance. "Or, rather, *he* was—Elliott."

As he had Saturday afternoon, Tom looked down upon the short figure, this time unobscured by a fanciful hat. He heard again in memory the distinctive timbre of a voice breaking—that of a boy on the cusp of becoming man. Elliott looked up at him now with apprehension. Even in the low light he could see a wisp of hair above her lip. This was a woman on the cusp of becoming a man.

"People were starting to gather," he explained. "So I asked on the off-chance if anyone knew who the victim might be, thinking someone might have seen the tall man going into the wood earlier. A short man supplied the answer.

"It was you, Elliott," Tom continued. "You were in breeches and a Cavalier's hat. You might have got the gear from Asda where you work. All the Halloween costumes were on display. But that's not important. What is, is that you were able to identify the victim—Charley Rouse. You knew him. But *how* did you know him?"

Tom knew the answer. Because in the caravan park Elliott had found herself, without warning, once again neighbour to Rouse, a frightening echo of her childhood.

Elliott bolted outside the confine of the yew canopy into the twilight of the churchyard, racing past the west porch of St. Nicholas's, now almost consumed in shadow, toward the hedge bordering the rise above the millpond.

"Elliott!" Barbara called, lifting her cassock, almost stumbling in her effort to run in the binding garb. Tom tore after her. The millpond beyond was cold and still, but deeper than it looked. He could not gauge the depth of Elliott's despair, what she might do.

He reached her first.

"Do you know," Elliott said, turning suddenly by the set of rickety wooden steps down to the millpond. "I think he only recognised me in the last moments of his miserable life, when he turned at the tree with this ... startled look on his ugly face before he turned back to ..." Her eyes blazed. "Yes, he looked at me at Buttles, but he didn't see. He didn't see!"

"You're older, darling" Barbara came up behind, panting softy. "You're not the child you were. And you're starting a transformation.

"He wasn't interested in *looking* at me!" Elliott spat. "He didn't even really look at Dania, the pig. Not properly like a husband, boyfriend, lover, whatever he is! He only had eyes for Lily. I could see him *watching* her in that way, the sly touches, the slow seduction. I overheard him calling Lily his 'ladyfriend' to someone in the park. I wanted to vomit. And Dania hadn't a clue, not a clue!"

"I didn't either," Barbara's voice cracked.

"Oh, Barb, what did we know about anything in those days? And you weren't really around. How could you be? You've always been so much older, my big sister. Living your own life, trying to get away from the hell that was ours."

"The guilt ... " Barbara's words drowned in a sob.

"Lily is a beautiful child," Elliott's voice was fierce. "She's smart and funny and blooming with potential, and

95

had no idea what awaited her from someone she believes utterly kind and trustworthy." She paused. "So I decided—somehow—to put an end to it, to make sure she would be safe."

"And," Tom said, "you thought there might be an opportunity at the Battle of Thornford."

"I did. And there was."

Tom's ears pricked to the rumble of male voices near the church's west door, recognizing Blessing's drawl and Bliss's bark. Barbara's hand went to her sister's.

"Let me do this for you, Elise."

"Elliott, *please*, Barb."

"Let me do this for you." She pulled Elliott into her embrace.

It was Barbara who looked past Elliott's shoulder to Tom this time. He saw the supplicating shine in her eyes, lit by the moon, brighter and higher in the sky now. He had no healing words for her, and now he carried the burden of what he'd heard and what he'd seen. What he knew to be true.

Was that a faint "no" he heard from Elliott, weeping on Barbara's shoulder? He wasn't sure. Two figures emerged from shadow, faces set in grim lines, and posed the first of many questions.

7

Friday

A sudden shriek jolted Tom from somewhere deep in his ruminations and set Gloria—or, possibly, Powell—springing from among the midden of papers and books on his desk, nearly knocking over a half-filled water glass. He watched the cat tear through the open French doors into the back garden as the shriek became a fulminating roar.

"Mrs. Prowse!" he shouted, glancing at the time—7:06, *good God*—on his open laptop. "MRS. PROWSE!!" Miraculously the roar ebbed to a sad squeak like that of some dying squirrel. "Mrs. Prowse," he said as Madrun rounded her head into the open door of his study. "Must you?"

"*Someone*, Mr. Christmas," Madrun said, her glasses dropping down her nose, "has tracked mud on my good clean carpets."

"Oh dear."

"Quite distinct ones, I'd say. About a size ten shoe."

"As I share this house with two females, two cats and one dog, I think it's safe to say the tracks are mine."

"Indeed."

"It rained last night."

"Not until after eleven, Mr. Christmas."

Tom sighed. Dried mud there might be, but hoovering the rugs by his study door with her beloved BeastMaster Home Deluxe 5000 vacuum at an uncommonly early (or uncommonly late) hour was not unknown when Madrun was possessed by the devil's own curiosity on some matter or other—and he could guess what it was in this instance.

"I was out late," he said.

"The quiz ended before ten."

"So it did."

If this were chess with his Honorary Father—Tom glanced at the email he was composing to the Reverend Canon Christopher Holdsworth who had stood *in loco patris* for him during his upbringing by two (wonderful!) women—this would surely be stalemate.

Madrun, rarely stalemated, ploughed on: "Who won?"

"The Irregulars." When he arrived at Totnes Police Station, Tom had read the confirmation text on his phone, one of several from Mark (including *Where are you? Are you all right?* and *We'll carry on then, shall we?*). But it was Jago to whom he sent a text, a more meaningful one.

"And the winning question?"

"I don't know." Tom felt checkmated. "Mrs. Prowse, before we go round the mulberry bush one more time: I expect you haven't spoken with Jago."

"He won't answer his phone."

"It is—" he glanced again at his computer—"7:08 in the morning. Many people don't care to be—"

"He does get calls for tows and the like early in the morning, Mr. Christmas."

"Yes, I know, but ..." *Undoubtedly Jago opened one*

*bleary eye, clocked his caller on the screen, and turned over in
bed.* "Anyway, I can tell you this much: any ancient worry
you may have had about Jago is baseless." He was certain
some village curtain-twitcher—most likely Madrun's great
friend Karla Skynner from her perch over the post office—
had alerted her to last evening's curious parade of priests
and police between pub and churchyard. "And, if there are
others in the village who have been giving wide berth to
Jago these last several years, they can stop."

He was gratified to see Madrun's stolid expression
soften a little. Brother and sister had a sort of prickly relationship, the ins and outs of which he hadn't quite navigated.
He was more astonished with what she *didn't* ask.

"But," he added quickly, before she *did* ask, "I'm afraid
there may be unintended and cheerless consequences
for some people in the village." Sharon Pearce and her
child-minding business, for one, slipped into his mind,
not to mention those who suffered Rouse's unwanted
attentions as children. "I think you know what I mean.
And Mrs. Prowse," he hurried on, "I could murder a cup
of coffee, if you don't mind making me one."

He immediately regretted his choice of words.
Madrun, fortunately, appeared sufficiently diverted.

"Have you had nothing to eat?" She frowned, glancing
around his desk.

"Coffee's all I need." Tom raised a warning hand.
"Please, Mrs. Prowse, no homilies on the importance of
breakfast. And, please, no more hoovering. At least for
another hour."

Tom yawned deeply—he had had a very poor sleep—and
turned back to his screen to reread what he had written.
DI Bliss and DS Blessing, he had summarized for Chris,

99

had been entirely focused on Barbara, ignoring Elliott, granting him, Tom, only a cursory nod. She was the beneficiary of police-speak boilerplate—an invitation to "help us with our enquiries." The undertone was invidious and the request, of course, unwisely refused. *Why now*, Tom had had the impertinence to ask, the pub quiz looming suddenly, ludicrously, important, a futile way to spare Barbara ordeal, if only for an hour. The detectives' expressions were unreadable in the twilit graveyard, but their silence was. Barbara, despite earlier valiance, seemed to shrink beside their bulky forms. A beam of light from a new moon rising over the millpond penetrated her glasses and captured the uncertainty in her eyes. As Barbara was led away up the path, Elliott stood rigid, staring after her sister in what Tom interpreted as mute horror. He returned to the Reverend Canon's email.

> I was utterly torn. My first impulse was to tear after them and tell them they were well wide of the mark, though I knew from past experience (which I've mentioned before) that the two detectives could be awfully adept at single-mindedness. But I didn't, or some conflicting impulse stopped me, and the moment was lost. I was left in the company of a confessed murderer, and though the gruesome image of Charley Rouse in death had not left me, my heart nevertheless strayed to another victim, his victim, the woman before me (or 'man', perhaps I should write? I'm uncertain of the correct language) who had chosen such a wrongful path to justice and resolution.

Tom's mind returned once again to the previous evening. *What are you going to do,* he had asked Elliott, finally shaking her by the shoulders to free her from her momentary fugue state. Focus returned to Elliott's eyes, a look flashed across her face that Tom couldn't interpret, and like a rocket she was off, on feet swifter than Tom's middle-aged trotters. Tom called after her as he gave chase, but it was futile. A motorcycle roared into life somewhere off Church Walk—Elliott's, presumably—and Tom witnessed with dismay a single red taillight vanish into the shadows down Pennycross Road as he dashed to the vicarage to fetch his car keys from the boot room peg. There was no point in chasing after Elliott. Who knew where she was going? Perhaps she was fleeing the county. It was Barbara who needed his help.

I know it's only 15 minutes to town, but the drive seemed agonizingly long. My mind roiled. I knew what was true. (I had no reason to think Elliott was some sort of fantasist). But what would I do at Totnes Police Station with what I knew? Tell on Elliott Coaker? (When I was a boy one of the worst things was being a grass.) Or should I keep my counsel? But Elliott had taken the life of a fellow human being! So much of my waffling was driven by my repugnance for Charley's crimes against children. What was more important—compassion or justice? Justice for the murdered man? Justice for the abused children? Compassion for the murderer? Compassion for the victims? You once said to me that when we are children, and innocent, we love justice, but when we are adults, and guilty of many transgressions, we prefer mercy. I think somewhere in my heart of hearts I wanted Elliott to go free.

But what then of Barbara? Suffer for something she didn't do?

Of course, I know a confession is only one part of evidence. *Corpus delicti* and all that. There has to be something admissible in court apart from a confession. But Barbara had handled the murder weapon. Traces of blood would be on her clothes. That was damning evidence. How could it not be damning evidence? I was certain there was no collusion between the two siblings in this crime. But Barbara had surely been keeping her eye on Elliott, ready to swoop in and clean up if necessary. What if each of the two confessed to the crime? If the Crown couldn't prove which one was responsible, might there be reasonable doubt and they would go free? Did I want that? And what of me? If the truth later emerged, could I be charged with perverting the course of justice for what I <u>didn't</u> do when I should have done something? Pardon these scrambled early morning thoughts, Chris! I'd been preparing a sermon this week about the limits of forgiveness. I think I have some additional material.

Tom thought back to his arrival at the police station, a utilitarian assembly of dark brown brick likely built in the hard years after the war, darker still with last light falling over Totnes and black clouds advancing on the moon. As he passed into the reception area, he was assailed by an aroma that in other circumstances would have had him salivating, but now made his stomach lurch. Behind a desk a young constable was shovelling curry into his face like a boy in an orphan's home, eyes fixed at something on his desk out of Tom's view—his iPhone, most likely.

"Yes, you can help me," Tom said impatiently, after a moment watching the spoon round its way between open mouth and plastic container.

The constable gurgled something, reached for a serviette and swiped it across his lips. He turned his head and glanced down at Tom's clerical collar. "Another one," he said with mild surprise.

"Another…? Is the other one still here?"

"What's a collective of vicars called then, I wonder?"

"A prudence, a prudence of vicars," Tom replied wearily. "But I'm not sure two of anything constitutes a collective." He had a sudden thought. Had Barbara placed a call to the diocesan office seeking a proctor? Asking for legal assistance at this stage would be an ominous sign. "There aren't more than two of us here, are there?"

"No. You're the only other one." He wiped his mouth again and affected a professional smile. "So, how can I help you, Vicar?"

Tom stared numbly at the constable's square, ruddy, freckled face, the spawning of generations of West Country farmers.

I need to speak with DI Bliss or DS Blessing on an urgent matter.

Oh, I'm just here to collect a colleague of mine.
I'd like to report a missing dog.
Do you know the way to San Jose?
"Vicar?" the constable prompted.
"I—"

I had opened my mouth, uncertain of what
shape my words would take, when the bass
throb of an approaching motorcycle outside
distracted me. The constable prompted me
once again, but a small figure, helmet in
hand, pushed through the doors. We both
turned to look. It was Elliott, as I hoped it
would be. I don't know how to describe
the expression on her pale face. Frightened?
Resolute? Sad? Can it be all those at once?
Where have you been? I asked, drawing her
away from the constable's hearing to the
visitors' bench. To talk with Danka, she
said. To speak with her first, she amended.
And what did you tell her? The truth, she
replied, all of it. She blinked back tears. I
imagined the conversation utterly harrow-
ing and gave her several moments to
compose herself. And what are you going
to do? I asked her as I had earlier in the
churchyard, this time with less vehemence
and greater expectation. After all, why was
she here? Elliott looked past me, to the
constable, to the doors leading to the depths
of the police station. The truth, she said.
And my truth is, I was enormously relieved
in that moment, and grateful in many ways,

not the least—and this is entirely selfish and unflattering—that I was relieved of having to make a choice. Of having to be involved.

Tom lifted his fingers from the keyboard, leaned back to reread what he had written, and made some small amendments to clue Chris to the *dramatis personae*. He didn't feel wholly happy with himself, as though he had failed a test of courage, but there was little he could do about it now, other than offer prayers for all and sundry in this tragic event, not excluding himself. He looked up as Madrun bustled into his study with a tray bearing a cafetière, a coffee cup—and a plate of almond biscuits, for which he admitted (to himself) he was grateful. His stomach growled.

"I do apologize for the muck on the carpetting," he said as he cleared a space on his desk for the tray. "When I got back last night—well, early this morning—I found someone had left a car in Poynton Shute blocking the entrance to our drive, so I parked near the church and came through the back garden. I couldn't find my torch in the car so I must have stumbled into one of the flowerbeds on the way."

"And came though there," Madrun nodded toward the French doors, "which," she continued crisply, "you had not locked earlier, went through to the kitchen to fetch a glass of water," she gestured to the half-empty glass as she set down the tray, "trailing mud, returned here, and fell asleep on that couch—the afghan's in a heap—though you have a perfectly fine made-up bed upstairs."

"Worthy of Sherlock Holmes, Mrs. Prowse." He pressed down the cafetière's plunger with one hand. "I'd had a notion of jotting down my thoughts quickly, but sleep—"

"You are also wearing yesterday's clothes and you are unshaven."

"So I am." Tom ran his other hand over bristly flesh, his finger landing on the scars of the earlier cuts. He was reminded, for a flash, of his heartrending conversation with Barbara in the car as he drove her home after her interrogation through pounding rain to Hamlyn Ferrers. It had been the excess of blood dripping from her folded surplice, noted by the St. John's Ambulance attendant, that had amplified police conjecture. "You used it to blot the blood, didn't you," Tom said to her, "deliberately, to draw greater attention to yourself, should suspicion supplant acceptance that Rouse's death was mere accident." Her silence had been assent. He wondered at her willingness to sacrifice herself for her sibling, at the burden of guilt she carried for Elise/Elliott's suffering. He would write these things to Chris, in a few minutes, after the coffee and biscuits had worked their wonders.

Madrun's eyebrows arched. "Charley Rouse was murdered then, I take it."

"Yes, Mrs. Prowse, he was."

"And who…?"

"Did this terrible thing?" The answer would be the talk of the washhouse before long, with all the attendant speculation. But, as ever, he didn't want the vicarage to be the tittle-tattle equivalent of the Broad Street pump. "You'll find out soon enough, Mrs. Prowse."

Acknowledgments

My thanks to Matt Joudrey for suggesting a noncanonical Father Christmas adventure, and to Karen Clavelle for her perspicacious editing. Thanks, too, to Sandra Vincent, Spencer Holmes and Perry Holmes for some early reflections on these scribblings.

C.C. Benison is the nom de plume of Doug Whiteway. His first book, *Death at Buckingham Palace* won the Arthur Ellis Award for Best First Novel, and was followed by others in the "Her Majesty Investigates" series. He followed that series with the Father Christmas mysteries, featuring, as amateur sleuth, the vicar of the English village of Thornford Regis, Tom Christmas. Titles include *Twelve Drummers Drumming, Eleven Pipers Piping and Ten Lords A-Leaping*. His most recent novel is *Paul is Dead*, a psychological thriller. Benison lives in Winnipeg.